# THE MEMORY THIEVES

Ms Ferryman's lips pursed and she let out a soft sigh. "It's okay, Jonquil. Everything will be fine. You agreed to come here so you could escape whatever it was that happened to you. To forget and stop the pain. Isn't that so?"

Jonquil rubbed her nose and nodded.

"We'll help you with that, I promise. But you have to help us to help you. And that means letting go. It means letting go of time, of who you were – of everything. Are you willing to do that?"

ALSO BY DARREN SIMPSON

SCAVENGERS

# THE MEMORY THIEVES

## DARREN SIMPSON

USBORNE

For anyone who's hurting.

First published in the UK in 2021 by Usborne Publishing Ltd., Usborne House, 83-85 Saffron Hill, London EC1N 8RT, England. usborne.com
Usborne Verlag, Usborne Publishing Ltd., Prüfeninger Str. 20, 93049 Regensburg, Deutschland, VK Nr. 17560

Text copyright © Darren Simpson, 2021

The right of Darren Simpson to be identified as the author of this work has been asserted by him in accordance with the Copyright, Designs and Patents Act, 1988.

Illustration by Matt Saunders © Usborne Publishing Ltd. 2021

The name Usborne and the Balloon logo are Trade Marks of Usborne Publishing Ltd.

A CIP catalogue record for this book is available from the British Library.

ISBN 9781474976695  05774/1  JFMAM JASOND/21

Printed and bound in Great Britain by CPI Group (UK) Ltd, Croydon, CR0 4YY.

# WHAT YOU DON'T
# REMEMBER
# CAN'T HURT YOU

TREATMENT PHASE A

# TALL BONES

Cyan sat back against a huge curving rib. He was surrounded by a boundary of bone: a whale's yellowing skeleton, stranded in the sand. His creased uniform stood out against the dunes, like a green bottle on a deserted beach.

Taking a book from his satchel, Cyan found his page and plucked out his bookmark. He began to read, and was a few pages in when he heard a throbbing in the air.

He swept his white fringe from his tortoiseshell glasses, got up and peered through a gap between some ribs. Apart from outcrops of rock and some stranded, rusting boats, the landscape was all sandy knolls, topped here and there by patches of beach grass.

Cyan's gaze rose and he found the sound's source. An orange blip was cutting through the sky, coming in from the south and heading for the sanctuary. As the chopping of rotor blades sharpened, the helicopter took shape. The lights on its underbelly winked against a backdrop of cloud.

A muffled beep came from the pocket of Cyan's green trousers. He reached in and pulled out a small silver locket. With its thin chain still clipped to his trousers, he opened it up and read the message on its screen:

*Ms Ferryman's office. ASAP.*

Cyan sighed and slipped his bookmark back into his book. While grabbing his satchel, it knocked a clump of sand from a rib and something caught his eye. He paused, then got to his knees to brush more sand away.

Something had been scratched low into the bone. Tiny words, careful and deep.

*best to deceive the memory thieves*
*between green and red, fight don't forget*
S-7270

Cyan frowned. In all the time he'd spent at these bones, he'd never noticed this. The etched words and numbers were strange. Half of them didn't mean anything, and those that did sent an uncomfortable flutter through his stomach.

*memory thieves*
*fight don't forget*

Cyan brooded on the words while putting his book back in his satchel. Turning away, he left through the whale's parted jaws and mounted the quad bike parked on some nearby beach grass.

Cyan slapped on some goggles and flicked the ignition switch; all silence was lost to the engine's loud growls.

A twist of the throttle sent him racing across dunes. His blazer and shirt flapped wildly in the wind, and the hurtling quad spat sand in its wake.

He could see his destination up ahead, breaking the sandscape's monotony: the green hills of a grassy cove. To his right he saw several ships, half-buried and clustered around juts of rock. Some of the boats had tipped onto their sides, with their tall masts tilting towards the ground.

The clouds parted and sunlight hit the wrecks, causing the salt in their rust to sparkle like diamonds. Cyan grinned at the sight. He could taste the salty grit that hit his teeth. Revving the engine, he launched himself over another dune and laughed giddily when the quad landed with a thump.

Up ahead, two stone piers stretched like pincers from the cove's harbour. Tucked within the cove was the Elsewhere Sanctuary – a vast cube of white concrete, pocked with rows of large porthole windows.

Cyan passed the lighthouse on the eastern pier's tip. Its black-on-white spirals were thick but flaking, and its lantern panes were hidden behind slats, just as they'd been for as long as he could remember.

He revved the quad up the wide, cobbled ramp that led from the sand to the harbour's raised bank. A fellow resident leaped aside as he flew over the ramp's top. Cyan hit the brakes, swerving to a stop before grinning at his friend. "Ahoy, Teal!"

Teal grimaced and threw both hands into the air. "Can't you watch where you're going, Cyan?"

Cyan laughed. "Can't *you* watch where I'm going?"

Teal yanked off his wire spectacles and, after wiping them clean with his own green blazer, pinched the tape wrapped tightly around their bridge. "Worst driver on the island, I swear. Your quad's throwing dirt all over the place." He put the glasses back on and started scratching his neck and afro. "It's in my shirt and hair and…argh, *everywhere!*"

"Lighten up, joy boy. You've been here…however long, and you're still not used to a bit of sand?"

"I *hate* the sand."

"You love it. Gives you something to moan about."

"I've got you, Cyan; I'll always have something to moan about."

Cyan clicked his fingers. "Hey, did you see the helicopter come in?"

"Heard it land." Teal gestured over his shoulder to the hangar next to the sanctuary. Cyan could see the helicopter on the hangar's roof, motionless and gleaming on its helipad.

Teal shrugged. "Probably bringing in medical supplies or something."

"Supplies come with the hovercraft. I think it's a new resident." Cyan flicked dirt from his blazer's double-striped cuffs, then pulled his locket from his pocket. "Got a message to see Ms Ferryman. Maybe I'm doing a new resident's induction."

Teal shook his head. "Doubt it. We had Pewter come in just the other day. New residents don't come in that often."

"Dunno. There's always someone else who…wants to forget." Cyan slowed as he spoke, thinking back to the words he'd seen carved into bone. His eyebrows began to sink.

Teal shook his head again. "Nah. Not today."

Cyan's grin returned. "You're so sure of yourself! Okay, tell you what: I'll *bet* you it's a new resident."

"Oh, yeah? And what'll you bet?"

"Tonight's pudding."

Teal mulled this over and began stroking the small pot of his belly. "Deal. But don't whine when I'm eating your afters."

"Ditto. Sometime-somewhere!" Cyan doffed an imaginary cap, then shot across the harbour to whip through the hangar's double doors.

The quad's snarls echoed across steel walls, until Cyan parked by some other bikes and killed the engine. He hung his goggles on the handlebar and hopped off his seat. Smells of diesel and cool metal filled his nose.

Two mechanics were tinkering with the orange hovercraft that filled the hangar's bulk. Cyan saluted when they looked at him from behind massive twin propellers, then left the hangar and made for the sanctuary.

Hopping up the marble steps that scaled the staff floor and led to the sanctuary's entrance, Cyan paused to murmur beneath his breath: "S seven two seventy. Between green and red, fight don't…forget."

The words bothered him, though he couldn't put his finger on why.

A sudden flush of heat had him loosening his collar. He shook his head as if shaking the words away and – after stamping sand from his plimsolls – forced the spring back into his step.

And with a push of the revolving door, Cyan entered the Elsewhere Sanctuary.

# THE GRINDING DRAWER

Inside, at least twenty young residents – all dressed in the same green uniform – filled the sanctuary's foyer with chatter. Some crossed the blue carpet on their way to other rooms, while others sat together on trim, colourfully cushioned benches.

Paintings of ships and sailors decked the smooth oak walls. From its position between two spiral stairways, a large white clock faced the entrance, as if on vigilant watch. Its numbers were made of brass and – just like all the sanctuary's clocks – this clock had no hands. Its centre bore only the sanctuary's emblem: a simple, upside-down anchor within a ring of rope. The same emblem appeared on the breast of Cyan's blazer, on his satchel's clasp and on the casing of his locket.

Cyan headed for the corridor to the right and stopped at a door with a brass nameplate: *Ms Ferryman, Head Orderly*.

After knocking, he tucked his loose shirt into his trousers. There was a buzz from the electronic lock, and he eased the door open.

"Ahoy, Ms Ferryman."

Ms Ferryman beckoned from behind her desk, which had the same style as much of the sanctuary's furniture, with shallow drawers and jutting, tapered legs.

Someone was sitting on the chair that faced Ms Ferryman's desk; someone new and already in uniform.

The girl turned to study him with deep brown eyes. Her black, centre-parted hair was thick and wavy, and so long that it reached her hips. She had brown skin and looked a tad younger than himself – maybe about thirteen – though he wasn't sure of his own age.

While the girl watched him, Cyan saw a glimmer in her gaze: something like unease, perhaps even fear.

Ms Ferryman nudged the bun of black braids at the back of her head, waiting for the door to close and lock behind him. "Sit down, Cyan." She nodded at the bench by the wall. Cyan took a seat.

Ms Ferryman eyed him with a coolness that verged on being frosty, then tugged the hem of her white tunic. "A new resident was flown in this afternoon." She addressed the girl, who was now gazing timidly at her lap. "Would you like to introduce yourself to Cyan?"

The girl looked at him again. Her face was long and

delicate, with high cheekbones that rose when she tried to smile. She massaged her fingers while she spoke. "Hi, Cyan. I'm Pri—"

"No," interrupted Ms Ferryman. She lifted her primly trimmed eyebrows. The dark skin of her forehead wrinkled. "Remember: that's not your name any more. It's crucial to the treatment that you never use your real – your *old* – name. Names are one of the hardest things to forget. You need to be thorough in aiding its removal. Now try again."

The girl nodded in meek apology, cleared her throat and did as she was told. "Hello, Cyan. I'm…Jonquil."

"Ahoy, Jonquil." Cyan gave a little wave before frowning at Ms Ferryman. "What colour's jonquil? Some sort of… purple or something?"

"Yellow," said Ms Ferryman.

"Right." Cyan nodded as if he'd known all along, then noticed the confusion on Jonquil's face. "We're all named after colours," he explained. "So, I'm Cyan. Which is kind of bluey green."

Jonquil still looked puzzled.

"Don't worry," he went on. "It gets easier. All the new residents soon settle in."

Jonquil's smile was faint but grateful. She seemed unaware of her fidgeting fingers.

Ms Ferryman cleared her throat. "Cyan's been with us for a long time, Jonquil. He'll show you how to entertain yourself here on the Island of Elsewhere. There's plenty to do – exploring the caves and wrecks and so on. And he'll accompany you while you begin treatment and find your way around the sanctuary. It can be a little…overwhelming at first. We find that new residents benefit from having someone more experienced around. To ease them in." Her dark eyes moved to Cyan. "You don't mind, do you, Cyan?"

"Not one bit, Ms Ferryman."

"Thank you. First things first, then. Dr Haven is expecting her. She'll need to record her oath and receive an initial course of treatment. Could you take her to his office, and then guide her through the next reconfiguration, so she knows how to stay safe whenever it happens?"

"Consider it done."

"Thank you. We'll schedule a reconfiguration for later. Now, Jonquil, I see you're wearing a watch."

Jonquil glanced at the watch on her wrist. "Yes, it was a present from—"

Ms Ferryman's hand shot up. "Again. No talking about the past. Not to anyone. It's a simple rule, and it's essential if you want to get what you came here for. Now give me your watch, please."

Jonquil took off the watch and – after a moment's hesitation – handed it over. Ms Ferryman held it at a distance between finger and thumb, as if it were dirty or dangerous.

"We don't do time here," she explained, standing up to reveal trousers as starched and white as her tunic.

Cyan glimpsed the staff card clipped to Ms Ferryman's waist and couldn't help smiling at its photo of her. He'd often thought it looked far friendlier than the real thing.

"Time is an anchor," continued Ms Ferryman. "It hinders the…*disorientation*, as we call it, that's crucial to the Lethe Method."

With that, she marched on flat white shoes to one of the wooden cabinets by the far wall. She opened its lowest drawer and tossed the watch in before slamming the drawer shut. The three of them listened while the drawer's mechanism ground the watch to pieces.

When Cyan looked at Jonquil again he froze. A bright sheen was trembling in her eyes. He shuffled along the bench for a better look, trying to recall when he'd last seen someone so close to crying. But nothing came to mind.

Ms Ferryman must have noticed too. Her lips pursed and she let out a soft sigh. "It's okay, Jonquil. Everything will be fine. You agreed to come here so you could escape whatever it was that happened to you. To forget and stop the pain. Isn't that so?"

Jonquil rubbed her nose and nodded.

"We'll help you with that, I promise. But you have to help *us* to help you. And that means letting go." She looked back towards the grinding drawer. "It means letting go of time, of who you were – of everything. Are you willing to do that?"

Jonquil's eyes grew moister. For a moment it looked like she might cry real, actual tears. But she blinked them away, pushed out her chest and nodded.

"Good. Then you'll find peace soon enough. We'll see to that."

There was a dull *thunk* as the watch – or whatever was left of it – dropped into the incinerator below.

Ms Ferryman opened another drawer, took something out and returned to her seat. She held the object – a metal circle no bigger than a coin, with a fine chain and clip attached to its side – in the light of her orb-like desk lamp.

"This is your locket. Every resident has one." She opened the locket to reveal its round, blank screen. "Your locket serves multiple functions. It replays your oath – something you'll be recording with Dr Haven shortly – whenever you need it. It acts as an alert system. It tells you when to get up, when to pick up your lunch and when to have dinner. These things will never happen at regular times, but between them and treatment sessions, you're free to do as you please. Your locket will also help you to navigate the sanctuary and find your way back when you're exploring the island. Have it with you at *all* times, and charge it using the charger in whichever bedroom it leads

20

you to at night. Here, take it. Use this clip to attach it firmly to the inside of your pocket."

Jonquil held the locket warily on her open palm, before clipping it in her skirt pocket.

Ms Ferryman said something, but Cyan didn't catch the words. He'd seen a flash through one of the large round windows set deep into the wall: a white flicker of flame. His hands gripped the bench, trembling and clawed, until he realized it was a trick of the light – the sun's reflection on a quad rider's goggles.

"Cyan?"

His eyes shifted to Ms Ferryman. He inhaled deeply, felt the tightness leaving his chest.

"I *said*," repeated Ms Ferryman, "you can take Jonquil to see Dr Haven now."

"Right." Cyan glanced at the window again, almost laughing with relief. He beamed and rubbed behind his ear. "Sure. Dr Haven."

Cyan and Jonquil rose from their seats. Cyan offered his hand, which Jonquil took shyly so he could lead her to the door.

He pressed the button that released its electric lock. While leaving, he pretended to doff a cap at Ms Ferryman. "Sometime-somewhere, Ms Ferryman."

"Same to you, Cyan." Ms Ferryman was already bending towards some paperwork on her desk.

Cyan led Jonquil across the foyer before stopping by its revolving door. "Okay, a bit of orientation first. Right now, we're on the communal floor, which is basically for everyone. This is the foyer – though you've probably figured that out for yourself. Dr Haven's office is that way, on the opposite side to Ms Ferryman's."

Jonquil frowned at the foyer's benches, floor lamps and potted plants. "All this furniture and stuff... It's like being in the past or something."

"Oh yeah? How far in the past?"

"I'm not sure. Sort of...1950s, I guess?"

"What year is it now?"

Jonquil gave a stunted laugh, then realized Cyan meant it. She began to reply but caught herself and snapped her mouth shut. "Ms Ferryman said I...can't talk about things like that."

Cyan grinned. "I know. Just testing." He shrugged. "I honestly have no idea what decade it is, but it doesn't matter. Like Ms Ferryman said, we don't really do time here." He waggled a thumb at the handless clock. "Days, months, even the seasons... It all blends."

He pointed at each of the four corridors joining the foyer. "So, these corridors'll take you to everything on this floor: lounge, games room, canteen, pool, library. And you see those stairs?" He clicked his fingers at the spiral staircases to each side of the clock. "They skip the next floor to get you to the rooms further up."

Jonquil considered each staircase. "Why skip the next floor?"

"It's the engine floor. Full of mechanisms for the upper rooms."

"Mechanisms?"

Cyan wriggled his white eyebrows. "You'll see. But basically, only staff can access the engine floor. Same goes for the floor below us. That's the staff floor, for staff living quarters, laundry, that sort of thing. I'll show you more later, but we'd better get to Dr Haven first. He'll be waiting for you."

"Who's Dr Haven?"

"The sanctuary's director. He oversees the treatment."

"What's he like?"

"Dresses like a funeral director and smells of soap, but he's nice enough. Do you usually do that?"

"Do what?"

"All that twiddling with your fingers. You're worse than Ruby. She can't stay still either."

Jonquil parted her hands, only to start playing with her hair instead. "Ruby?"

"You'll have the...*pleasure* –" Cyan made speech marks with his fingers – "soon enough. Sometime. Somewhere."

Cyan clocked a giant of a man leaving Dr Haven's office and started tugging Jonquil towards the corridor. "Mr Banter! Could you hold the door open?"

The blond, bespectacled orderly – with his white tunic taut against his muscly bulk – turned to see Cyan waving.

Jonquil spoke quietly, her lips barely moving. "Is that one of Ms Ferryman's orderlies?"

"Not quite. He's Dr Haven's personal orderly and assistant." Cyan lowered his voice. "Not blessed with the best bedside manner. Has all the charisma of a potato."

He grinned and waved again as they entered the corridor, but frowned when Mr Banter – smiling vaguely – let the door shut behind him.

The hulking orderly stayed where he was, blocking the way to Dr Haven's office.

Cyan shrugged. "Jonquil, meet Mr Banter. Mr Banter, this is Jonquil, a new resident."

Jonquil stared up at Mr Banter's eyes, which were grossly magnified by his glasses, bright blue beneath cropped, straw-blond hair.

"Hello, Mr Banter," croaked Jonquil.

The orderly let out a rumbling sigh. His smile edged towards a smirk.

"So, Mr Banter." Cyan shot a grin at Jonquil. "There appears to be a massive slab of person in our way. Would you mind moving? The director's expecting us."

After lifting a blond eyebrow, Mr Banter pivoted languidly on the spot and strode away.

"Thank you!" called Cyan, before whispering to Jonquil.

"Mr Banter's not one to waste words. Matter of fact, no one's ever heard him speak. But unlike the other residents, I don't think he's a mute. I just think he likes it that way."

Cyan knocked on the office door.

"Who is it?" came a mild voice from within.

"Cyan. I've got Jonquil to see you."

"Very good. One moment."

Cyan sensed Jonquil reaching out, almost touching the hair that hung against his cheek. He pulled gently away.

"Why is it so white?" asked Jonquil. "I've never seen anything like it. Not on someone your age."

Cyan shrugged. "Dunno. Why is sand the colour of sand?"

The voice came again from behind the door. "You can come in now."

# THE LETHE METHOD

The lock buzzed; Cyan pushed the door.

It opened with a faint waft of antiseptic, and revealed Dr Haven standing by his desk, dressed in his usual pinstriped grey trousers, charcoal waistcoat, pristine white shirt and long-tailed black coat. His shoes shone as slickly as his bald patch, which rose through the grey hair at the back and sides of his head.

"Good afternoon, Cyan." The doctor's voice was as warm as his smile. His gaze moved to Jonquil. "And you must be…"

"Pri—"

"*No.*" Cyan and Dr Haven interrupted together.

She corrected herself. "Jonquil. I'm Jonquil."

"That's right," said the doctor. "Welcome to the Elsewhere Sanctuary, Jonquil. I'm Dr Haven, the sanctuary's director. I'm also its resident doctor, for all aches and pains of the

**26**

body and mind." He tightened his grey tie, just a little, and gestured towards the chair facing his desk. "Please, come in. Make yourself comfortable."

Jonquil cast a glance at Cyan, who nodded encouragingly before following her into the room. He took a seat on the bench by the wall. The door locked itself with a click.

Jonquil sat down as instructed. Her eyes grew large while they roved, lost in the colours of the frames lining every wall. Butterflies were pinned behind the frames' glass panes, organized in neat, orderly rows.

"All these butterflies…" she began. "They're… beautiful."

Light from the windows was cast back into the room, reflected by a thousand fragile wings. Jonquil continued to turn her head, with butterfly hues drifting across her skin.

Dr Haven browsed one of the medicine cabinets at the far end of the office. "Yes. I suppose they are."

"But isn't pinning them up like that a bit…a little…" Jonquil trailed off.

Dr Haven turned to raise a friendly eyebrow. "Cruel?"

She nodded uncomfortably.

The director looked amused. "Not at all. They feel very little pain when they die. No more pain than a fly feels when you swat it with a newspaper. Do you feel bad for flies when they die? Or ants or cockroaches?"

"I…guess not."

"Then there you have it. It's best not to allow appearances to encourage prejudice. And do you know how long the average butterfly lives? Two weeks at most. There's not much to take away. And at least here –" he swirled a long, immaculate finger around the room – "they're preserved so we can always appreciate them. Now, Jonquil. Take these, please."

Dr Haven placed a small silver tray on the desk and slid it towards her. Jonquil stared at its contents: a glass of water, and a small paper cup filled with pills.

"There's nothing there that won't help you," assured the doctor. "Isn't that so, Cyan?"

Jonquil glanced again at Cyan. When he gave her a cheery thumbs up, she closed her eyes, tipped the pills into her mouth and washed them down.

Dr Haven restored the cup and glass to the tray. "Excellent. Now count to ten in your head." He waited for some moments. "All done? Good. Take this pen and sign these two forms, here and here. As soon as you're done, we'll record your oath."

Jonquil blinked at the forms as if struggling to focus. After swaying very slightly, she scrunched up her eyes, let out a slow breath and – somewhat limply – put pen to paper.

When she was finished, the doctor put the sheets in

a drawer and began fussing with a small metallic camera clamped to his desk.

Jonquil gazed at the camera's lens. "What's the oath?"

Dr Haven didn't look up. "Cyan, would you be so good as to explain?"

Cyan crouched next to Jonquil and took out his locket. "Here. This is mine." He opened the locket's front, held his thumb against its screen and spoke clearly into the device: "Oath."

The screen flickered to life to show an image of Cyan. In the video his hair was jet-black, apart from a white streak that ran along his parting. His eyes were red with tears and he was sitting in the very chair Jonquil was using now.

The recording of him sniffed and shuddered, pleading to the camera: "I want to forget… I *want*…to forget, okay? I never want to remember. *Never!*" His head dropped into his hands. The locket's screen went blank.

"Oh god," breathed Jonquil.

Cyan laughed and got up. "It's nothing, Jonquil. Whatever made me feel like that is long gone. And if I'm ever curious about what brought me here, I just watch this clip and – *poof!* – no more curiosity."

Dr Haven slipped a microchip into the desk's camera, then took his seat opposite Jonquil. "Thank you for that demonstration, Cyan. Now come behind me, please, so you're not in the camera's view."

With his elbows on the desk, the director leaned forward, joined the tips of his fingers, and looked Jonquil in the eye. "Jonquil. Without saying *anything* at all about it, please cast your mind back to the incident that caused you to seek solace here at our sanctuary. Give the episode some thought."

Jonquil's gaze sharpened. Some of the looseness left her shoulders and she frowned at her fretting fingers. "That's easy enough. I think about it all the time. I can't *not* think about it. What happened to me, what happened to—" She stopped herself, before going on. "I can't stop replaying it in my head. I can't stop the way it…it hurts."

Her voice had thickened, and her eyes began to brim, just as they'd done in Ms Ferryman's office. Cyan watched with his breath held, as fascinated by her tears as he was sorry for her pain.

"Everyone said it would," she croaked. "Everyone said the hurting would fade. But they're wrong. They have no idea. It *never* stops hurting. It just gets worse. That's why I'm here."

Dr Haven nodded, his voice soothing and kind. "But I'd like you to *really* think about what happened. Think about exact, specific details. Think about the sounds in your ears at the time. What you smelled, what the temperature was like. Think about how it felt for you. Try to remember those feelings: what went through your head, whether time froze or…accelerated. Think about your involvement – about any responsibility you had for what took place."

Tears were trickling freely down Jonquil's cheeks. Cyan looked on, torn between staring and looking away. The sight made the nape of his neck feel hot, and he hooked a finger through his collar to loosen it. The office felt suddenly way too warm.

Jonquil's nostrils twitched and flared. "I never—"

"*Don't*," cut in Dr Haven, "say anything about what happened. Merely think about it. And now, think about how much you want to forget."

Jonquil wiped her eyes with her sleeve. Her expression hardened. She nodded with a huff.

"Now tell the camera."

Jonquil glared at the lens. Her chest began to heave. "I want to forget. I. *Want*. To. Forget. I want it to go away. *For ever.*" Her gaze rose to Dr Haven, finally meeting his eyes. "Please," she begged. "Please make it go away."

The doctor nodded in approval. After handing Jonquil some tissues from a silver box on his desk, he got up, took the microchip from the camera and held it up to her. "Your oath is on this chip. Now, when you're ready, could you give me your locket?"

With her face hidden behind damp tissues, Jonquil fumbled at her skirt and handed him her locket.

Dr Haven removed its back and inserted the chip.

"That clip is there for you, Jonquil, whenever you need it." He handed the locket to her, then turned away. "And now we'll begin."

# THE STROBE CHAIR

Cyan saw Jonquil clench the locket in her hand. "Begin what?" she asked.

Dr Haven beckoned while he walked. "Today you'll receive just a short dose of strobe therapy."

"Strobe therapy?"

"Come this way."

He led her to a grey vinyl curtain in the corner and pulled it back to reveal what looked like a dentist's chair, with black leather cushioning and an angular chrome frame. But in place of the lamp that would usually cap a dental chair's arm, there was a concave glass screen.

"This is the strobe chair," said Dr Haven. "Please, take a seat."

Jonquil seemed reluctant. She remained where she was, standing by the chair. Cyan could see she was trembling.

When she turned her teary eyes to him, he beamed and

forced a sprightly nod. He couldn't wait to see her get better – to see her freed from whatever made her eyes well up that way.

Jonquil climbed on and lay back against the chair's stiff leather. Cyan eased some used tissues from her hand. When he offered a fresh one from the desk, she tried to smile and used it to dab what was left of her tears.

Cyan put a hand on her arm. "There's no need to be nervous. You won't feel a thing. Everything's going to get better, starting from now. It's not just time we don't do here. It's tears too."

He saw that she was clutching the chair's side, with the wet tissue clamped between her knuckles. Her breaths quickened when her eyes flitted to Dr Haven. "What does the chair do? You said something about…strobes."

The doctor was tapping at a console behind the chair. "I won't waste your time with technicalities, but I'll try to convey the basics."

He took two circular, metallic pads connected by wires to the console, and squirted some gel onto them before placing one on each of Jonquil's temples. She shuddered with their contact.

Dr Haven went on. "Beyond the Lethe Method, there are, of course…other ways to remove memory. Certain drugs can erase a patient's recollection of the last few days – or even a person's memory entirely. But this is all rather clumsy and doesn't allow the targeting of specific memories and their many associations. But the Lethe Method does, and this chair is the method's core.

"In its simplest terms, this screen here –" he adjusted the chair's arm so its screen hovered inches from Jonquil's nose – "sends rapid strobes into your vision. We call them strobes, but they're actually flickering images; images I've programmed myself using your resident's file – from the data we've gathered on your history and trauma."

He began to tap again at the console. "These images will flash by so quickly that you won't register them consciously. But they'll register at a deeper level. And with each stimulation, the pads on your temples will release electrical currents to…disrupt the triggered memory."

Jonquil tensed and moved to sit up, but the doctor eased her down with a gentle push of his finger. "Don't worry, Jonquil. There'll be no discomfort. The medication you took earlier will see to that, among other things…"

Jonquil's eyes flickered to Cyan. She looked as baffled as she did nervous, so he smiled, put a hand on her forearm and tried to explain.

"What Dr Haven means to say," he said, "is that – without you feeling a thing – this chair will bring up your horrible memories and zap them 'til they go away."

The director nodded. "Cyan has an…intriguing way with words, but he's got the right idea. The chair weakens targeted memories through regular stimulation and disruption. This works alongside the medication and disorientation you'll receive here at the sanctuary, which help to keep the memories at bay until they're finally removed. All in all, this constitutes the Lethe Method."

The doctor gazed serenely at the console. "Words can't do justice to how advanced the Lethe Method is, to be able to target memories with such laser-like accuracy. It's this that allows us to remove unwanted memories while preserving a patient's understanding of the world – of who they are within it."

The rise and fall of Jonquil's chest had slowed. Her breaths came long and deep. The pills were kicking in.

Her lips parted and she mumbled. "But what about…"

Cyan leaned in close. "About what?"

"The rules," she breathed. "Today… All those rules." She gazed ahead through heavy eyelids. "What if…I forget?"

Cyan patted her arm. "You won't. They never touch the memories you make here. They're not even allowed. They can only remove your old memories, from before you arrived."

Dr Haven nodded. "And rightly so. Here at the sanctuary we follow a strict ethical code. Memories formed on the island can't be touched. They're unrelated to your trauma. Influencing them isn't necessary to the treatment and therefore highly questionable."

Jonquil didn't seem to hear. She gawped blankly into the screen, with her chest barely moving. Cyan saw the tissue fall from her hand.

Dr Haven bent to study her pupils. "So, Jonquil. How are you feeling?"

Jonquil didn't respond. A small bead of saliva was pooling at the edge of her mouth.

"Good." Dr Haven went to tap the console screen again, but hesitated. Frowning abruptly, he rubbed his chin for several moments, nodded to himself, then tapped the screen a few more times.

After motioning Cyan away, he followed him and closed the vinyl curtain. "And how are you faring, Cyan?"

"Shipshape, thanks."

The chair hummed and ticked behind its curtain. Cyan heard a series of electronic clunks. Stuttering flashes began to illuminate the vinyl.

"Oh," began Cyan, remembering what he'd seen earlier. "I saw something interesting today. At the whale bones closest to the cove."

"And what would that be?"

"Words, scratched into one of the ribs. Something about –" Cyan looked down, trying to recall – "memory thieves. And fighting instead of forgetting. It was really weird. I mean, why would anyone write that?"

He lifted his eyes to Dr Haven, who was frowning and tapping his lips.

The doctor finally replied. "I have no idea." He gave a light tut and shrugged. "It sounds like gibberish to me. The nonsense graffiti of a bored resident, perhaps. I'd pay it no mind."

Flashes of light spilled over the curtain's top. Butterflies flickered as if fluttering in their frames.

The director continued. "Have you mentioned what you saw to anyone else?"

Cyan shook his head. "No."

"I'd suggest you keep it that way."

"How come?"

"Those words convey a somewhat…unhealthy sentiment, not helpful at all to the care we provide for residents. I mean –" the doctor's lips pursed with amusement – "why would anyone not want to forget? That's how we heal here. It's how residents recover from their traumas and tragedies. Which makes the whole… *memory thieves* thing absurd. I assume that's supposed to refer to our work at the sanctuary. But how can we steal memories that aren't wanted? How can it be thieving if we're removing something that causes suffering?"

Cyan chewed at his lower lip, deep in thought. "That's what I didn't get. It still felt kind of…weird, though."

"That's because it's illogical and confusing. Like I said:

nonsense. Nevertheless, it's nonsense best kept to yourself. It would be inconsiderate of you to tell anyone. Naturally there'd be…consequences."

Cyan's eyes went to the doctor. "Consequences?"

Dr Haven was watching the curtain. "I mean, there's no point in making anyone else feel uncomfortable, is there?"

Cyan considered this, thinking of his own discomfort over the etched message. He nodded. "Makes sense."

"Perfect sense." The doctor adjusted his grey tie. "But back to you, Cyan. What of your fear of fire? Is your pyrophobia improving?"

Cyan gave a gloomy shrug. "Comes and goes. I had a little panic today – first one in a while. I thought I saw a fire through the window. In Ms Ferryman's office."

Dr Haven nodded knowingly. "It was imaginary."

"Always is." Cyan looked glumly into the doctor's face. "It's still really scary when it happens, though. Every time I think I see fire—" He sucked in a deep breath and nodded at the vinyl curtain. "Is there really no way to…remove the fear?"

The director sighed. "I'm afraid not. Strobe therapy erases memories of the past, and your condition is unrelated to your history. It's an irrational fear, more common than you'd imagine; a phobia you've likely carried around since birth. We've been through this before, haven't we?"

Cyan stared at his plimsolls and shoved his hands into his blazer pockets.

The doctor continued. "But don't be downhearted. There are various therapies for pyrophobia and you're in the best place to receive them. I'll do everything I can to beat your condition, once and for all. We'll keep talking about it, and I'll continue to refine your medication. We'll get there eventually, Cyan. Just make sure you continue to avoid revealing it to anyone. Interference from others might—"

"Hinder our progress. Yeah, I know."

Cyan took his hands back out of his pockets. After managing to rustle up a smile, he spoke cheerily over the chair's clunks and clicks, nodding again at the curtain. "Jonquil seems nice, doesn't she? It'll be good when she's better."

Dr Haven smiled. "It most certainly will."

He cracked his knuckles, and the ceiling stuttered with light.

# BOOKS AND CHOCOLATE

Later, in the library, Cyan handed Jonquil a mug and set himself down beside her. They were sitting in sleek, low armchairs, not far from the library's wooden counter.

Cyan gestured at Jonquil's drink. "Fresh from the lounge. The sanctuary has the *best* hot chocolate. It'll perk you up in no time."

Jonquil gazed glassy-eyed into the mug, which she cradled in both hands.

"It's normal to be groggy after strobe therapy," said Cyan. "It passes soon enough. I always come here after my sessions. It's nice and quiet while you get your bearings back."

He closed his eyes, listening to the library's sounds: hushed words from staff at the counter; the soft padding of plimsolls across carpet.

When he heard the crackle of something burning, his

**41**

eyes opened and he whipped his head towards the sound. There was no fire, though; just a creak from a hanging wicker pod-chair. A resident was sitting cross-legged inside, propped up by bright cushions and lost in a book.

Cyan steadied his mug and waited for his pulse to settle down. He smiled at a slurp from Jonquil, nodding encouragingly. "Did you look around while I fetched your hot chocolate? It's a beautiful library, isn't it?"

Jonquil's eyelids fluttered. She peered past Cyan at curving lampshades and boldly patterned beanbags; cushioned hammocks between mahogany pillars; armchairs and loungers in dim, comfy nooks.

Some of the colour returned to Jonquil's face. Her pupils seemed to shrink. "If this is the library…where are the bookshelves?"

"Behind you." Cyan nodded at the tall cabinets looming in rows behind the counter. Their long shelves were protected by steel-framed doors, with glass panels revealing the spines of books.

When Jonquil twisted to stare, Cyan beamed with pride. "Ms Ferryman says books are milk and honey for the soul, which I think is spot on. And there's *loads* of time here for reading. That's one of the best things about the sanctuary."

Jonquil was looking at him with her head slightly tilted. "But why are the books all locked up like that?"

"Because there's a limit to the books you can take out."

"Isn't there always?"

"Not the number of books; the *type* of books. Each resident has certain books they're not allowed to read, in case they trigger…unwelcome memories. The last thing you want is a plot twist or character messing up your treatment."

Understanding began to dawn in Jonquil's eyes. "Oh."

"That's why they're all locked up like that. If you fancy getting a book out, you have to go to the counter and get an orderly to scan your locket. After that, they'll give you an electronic catalogue of the books you're allowed."

"Right…" Jonquil looked distracted. She was watching the library's other residents, who were nestled with novels in hammocks and chairs. "So you guys…have all forgotten stuff from your old lives, right?"

"Yup. All the bad stuff that's happened to us."

Jonquil's eyes were on Cyan. "Then how much of the world do you remember? I mean…" She sucked her upper lip. "Do these books make sense to you when you've forgotten about the world and…all the stuff that's in it? All the stuff that isn't here on the island?"

Cyan had to give this some thought. "Well, we still *sort* of remember things. It's like Dr Haven said: the treatment gets rid of the bad memories, but you keep your understanding of the world and how it works. So, all the stuff that's out there beyond the island – you know,

43

countries, sports, animals, stuff like that – it's all still in here." He tapped the side of his head. "But not in a way that's connected to our personal experience. It's sort of abstract, I guess. Detached." Cyan's forehead furrowed. He drummed his fingers against his mouth. "Does that make sense? Or am I talking rubbish?"

Jonquil sipped her chocolate, then began to nod slowly. "I *think* it makes sense. Sort of." Her eyes returned to the other residents. "So how many residents live at the sanctuary?"

"About a hundred or so. I think."

"And it's just young people?"

"Hm?"

"I haven't seen any adults in this uniform." She patted the lapel of her bottle-green blazer.

"Yeah, it's just kids and teenagers. The only adults here are staff. Been that way as far back as I can remember."

"How far back is that?"

"I don't have the foggiest. That's kind of the point here. It's—"

Cyan was interrupted by a chorus of muffled bleeps. Residents throughout the library reached for their lockets.

Cyan opened his own and clicked his tongue against the roof of his mouth. "A shuffle in thirty minutes. That'll be the one Ms Ferryman scheduled, so I can show you how to handle it safely."

Jonquil straightened on her seat. "I thought we were waiting for a…what was it…reconfiguration?"

"Same thing. We mostly call it a shuffle, much as it winds up Professor Vadasz. You'll meet him soon enough." He pointed with both hands at the library's exit. "Finish your drink. We'd better get going."

They were soon in the foyer, at the foot of the staircase to the right of the handless clock.

Cyan drummed his palms on his trousers. "Okay, Jonquil. You lead the way."

"The way?"

He nodded at the coiling flight of steps. "To the upper rooms. Anywhere up there you want."

"Anywhere at all?"

"Sure. Doesn't have much effect on where we'll end up."

Jonquil tipped her head to one side. "I don't understand."

Cyan's eyebrows wriggled behind his chunky glasses. "You will. Just get up there and go wherever you want. Have a quick look around. I'll follow."

"Quick?" Jonquil's brown eyes twinkled. Her lip began to curl. "Think you can keep up?"

"Sure I can. I'm—"

Jonquil was already up several steps. Cyan grabbed the rail and followed, with the foyer disappearing below him.

After passing the oak walls that hid the engine floor from the stairway, he hopped off the top step and hit the carpet of the upper rooms' first floor.

Jonquil was waiting for him in a wide hallway – a cube-shaped space with dark, wood-panelled walls. She turned to take in its thick rugs and the colourful fish paintings on the walls, then looked at the doors facing each other from the room's opposite ends. Each one of them had a small porthole window. "So I'm just going anywhere?"

"Anywhere. Makes no—"

She was off again.

Cyan trailed behind while Jonquil raced through hallways and up and down spiral staircases. Other residents sometimes had to hop aside, so that they bumped against tall plants and bronze lamps.

"Slow down!" panted Cyan. "Man alive – you're really fast!"

Jonquil showed no sign of slowing. "Thanks! I used to be a—"

"*Don't*…say more…"

"Sorry!"

"But seriously…slow down. Need…to show you… something."

Jonquil stopped and Cyan stumbled into her. He stooped for some moments with his hands on his knees, so that his white fringe hung over his face. After getting his breath back, he straightened and patted his chest. "Right. Okay… While you were running, did you hear your locket beeping? Three separate times?"

"Yeah. There was one just now."

"That's the countdown. Five minutes left until the shuffle starts. Notice anything about the hallways and staircases you've been whizzing around? And the bedrooms you've seen through open doors. Anything they've all got in common?"

Jonquil studied the hallway they were in. "The walls are all wooden. And they all have the same shape. Like big cubes."

"That's right. The rooms are all cubes. That's how it works – how the upper rooms move."

"What?"

"You've seen those puzzles, right? The flat ones where you have to slide plastic tiles around to make a picture."

Jonquil eyed him cynically. "Yeah, I know the ones."

Cyan used his fingers to make a square shape. "Now imagine one of those puzzles, but in 3-D. What would those moving tiles be in 3-D?"

"I guess…cubes?"

"Bullseye. And that's how these bedrooms and hallways move around; like cubes in a giant sliding puzzle."

Jonquil's eyes searched the walls. "I don't believe you."

Cyan laughed and carried on. "And those cubes need

a grid to move around in, right? That's what this is part of."
His finger traced the room's broad ebony trim, which
skirted the twelve edges of the floor, ceiling and walls.

"This border is part of the upper rooms' framework –
the huge grid that holds all the cubes in place. It also lets
the walls slide in all directions while the rooms – their
floors and ceilings and whatever's in them – go wherever
they're sent. So during a shuffle there's stuff moving all
over the place, but the framework stays put. That's why it's
the safest place to be.

"So basically, if your locket tells you a shuffle's coming
and you're up here, you need to get safely into the frame
before it all kicks off. Here." Cyan pointed at the hollows
in each vertical section of the room's frame. "These are
called snugs, okay? They're for residents and staff during
shuffles." Both of their lockets were beeping regularly now.
"Quick, get into one."

Jonquil shook her head. "This is ridiculous. You're having
me on." Even so, and with a look of mounting worry on her
face, Jonquil reversed cautiously into one of the snugs.

Cyan tucked himself into the opposite snug and gave
her two thumbs up. "There's nothing to worry about,
Jonquil. You're perfectly safe, as long as you stay in your
snug. Have you noticed the beeping's getting faster?"

Jonquil was as pale as she'd been before her hot
chocolate. She nodded wordlessly.

"And you feel that faint trembling?" Cyan had to raise his voice while the noise grew louder. He could hear it travelling up from the engine floor, reverberating through the framework – the gnash of cogs, the squeal of pulleys.

Cyan's heartbeat quickened. A laugh began to rise in his throat, but when it failed to reach his mouth he frowned. Something was sucking the joy out of this shuffle.

He pouted slightly, suddenly deep in thought. When he realized it was the message he'd found on the whale bones – that those words still niggled him more than he'd liked to admit – his frown deepened.

Jonquil shrieked across the rising din. "What is it?" Her eyes darted nervously left and right. "Is something wrong?"

Cyan pushed the thought aside. The walls thrummed and trembled around them, and he forced a giddy cackle through his lips. "It's all great!" he shouted. "Just stay put 'til it's over! Heeeeere it comes!"

# RECONFIGURATION

The floor beyond the frame's edge fell away, followed swiftly by the room's descending ceiling. Cyan caught sight of Jonquil's widening eyes, before a wall slid along the frame's grooves to block his view. When it was gone, he managed to shout a quick, "It's okay!" before another wall shot up from below.

Wooden walls – many of them with doors – flew by with increasing speed, from top to bottom and bottom to top, left to right and right to left. Cyan saw staircases, bedrooms and hallways, all coasting through the space within the cube-shaped frame, most of them on the cusp of collision with sliding walls.

On it went with a thunderous rumble – with an exhilarating grind and relentless squeal. And with every passing room, Cyan glimpsed floors and ceilings, wardrobes and beds; beanbags and tables, mirrors and shelves; quaking plants and nodding lamps; fat bright cushions and vivid fluffy rugs… On and on, lurching and sliding, until the movements began to slow.

The noise gradually fell in volume, and when everything finally slotted into place, Cyan and Jonquil found themselves looking into a new hallway with a spiral staircase in its centre.

Cyan left his snug and passed the stairs. "You all right?" He offered a hand to Jonquil, who clutched it and allowed herself to be pulled from her hollow. Cyan felt the trembling in her arms.

She looked anxiously around the room, her grip still tight on Cyan's fingers. "We're…" Her voice was hoarse. "We've been moved. Moved to…somewhere…"

Cyan scratched the back of his neck. "Not technically. We're still in the same part of the framework. It doesn't move, remember? But, yeah, a different room's been moved to us. Every room and hallway up here'll be different now. There's no going back the way you came. It's all been rearranged."

Jonquil gawped at each of the walls now surrounding them. Her brow furrowed. "So how *do* we get back? How do we find our way to the foyer?"

"Open your locket. Okay, now keep your thumb on the screen and say 'foyer'."

Jonquil did so.

Cyan pointed at her screen. "See that green arrow?

That's basically a compass. It'll take you along the quickest route to wherever you say you want to go. But if you're ever wandering around these floors and hear a buzz from your locket, check there's not a red cross pointing where you're heading."

"What's a red cross mean?"

"No-zones. I'll show you."

With Cyan holding her hand and ahoying any residents they passed, they drifted through cubic corridors and up and down staircases, until their lockets buzzed suddenly in unison.

"There we go." Cyan pointed at the red cross on Jonquil's screen. He tapped one of its four arms, which was slightly longer than the rest. Then he pivoted Jonquil so that the cross revolved like a compass needle, pointing at a door ahead. "So, all the places we've been so far have been go-zones – places that are safe to walk. But this little cross warns you there's a no-zone behind that door."

Jonquil took a step back. "What's a no-zone? Is it dangerous?"

"Only if you're a moron. Go on, have a look." He nudged her gently forward.

"You sure it's safe?"

"Sure I'm sure. Just hold on to the door frame and keep your feet in *this* room. Go on." Cyan smiled and put a hand on her back. "I promise it's safe."

Jonquil's locket buzzed more angrily with every step she took. While holding the door frame with one hand, she eased the door open.

Cyan saw her grip tighten. He crossed the room and peered over her shoulder at the floorless space beyond the door.

There was a distant ceiling about two storeys above. The drop from where they stood was several storeys down. Cyan could see some exposed bedrooms and hallways, each bordering this huge shaft of hollow space.

Faint sounds echoed through the emptiness: scuffing footsteps from nearby rooms; muffled snippets of conversation; creaks and groans from the ebony framework.

"*That*," said Cyan, "is a no-zone."

"But that's just...*ludicrous*. It's so dangerous." Jonquil pointed down into the emptiness. "Look. Those rooms don't even have walls to protect people from that fall."

"Yep. But the lockets won't let residents anywhere near them. Just like yours didn't want you to go near this door."

It took some time for Jonquil to speak. "But this...no-zone... Why's it even here?"

"Needs to be. Think of those puzzles with the sliding tiles again. They always have an empty space, right? What's it for?"

Jonquil was retreating from the door. "To make room to move tiles."

"Top marks." Cyan let the door close. "And that's what no-zones are. Empty spaces to allow the filled spaces to move."

"I think I'm going to be sick."

Cyan snorted, but his smirk disappeared. "Hang on. You mean it?"

Jonquil stooped and clutched her belly. "I just need… to sit down."

"Man alive…" Cyan glanced about before speaking into his locket. "Bathroom." He frowned at its screen. "It's a bit of a trek to the loos. They're always at the edges of each floor; can't move 'cos of the plumbing or whatever. But we went past a bedroom a second ago. It had its door open. We'll go there and find somewhere to sit. And some sort of puke vessel. Just in case. Will you make it?"

Jonquil nodded and Cyan led her through a hallway. They entered a bedroom, where two men in grey boiler suits were lugging a chest of drawers and clipping it to the floor.

After making Jonquil sit on the bed's edge, Cyan handed her a bin. "Just in case."

She clutched it to her chest as if holding on for dear life.

The men in boiler suits looked on impassively. One of them spoke while placing a draughts set on top of the drawers. "New resident?"

Cyan clicked his fingers. "Got it in one."

The second man piped up. "She'll get used to it. They all do."

"Yup." Cyan sat on the bed next to Jonquil. "By the way, if you have to spew, I'm only holding your hair back if you promise to miss my fingers. Deal?"

Jonquil took a shuddering breath. "Deal."

"That's a smell you just can't wash away. Not even with a million years of scrubbing. You know what I mean?" He pulled a face. "Just *thinking* of that sick smell... Bleurgh. It's enough to make me throw up right now. Like—"

"I said *deal*."

One of the men chuckled. "Cyan takes some getting used to as well."

Jonquil looked up from her bin to watch the men get on with their business. They were moving about the room, swapping its furnishings with others laid out on a trolley. One of them hung a picture of a sea-straddling rainbow above the bed, while the other set a box of elaborate wooden puzzles on the floor.

"What are they doing?" asked Jonquil.

Cyan watched them too. "Well, it's not just rooms that move around in the sanctuary. Things within the rooms move too. Even on the communal floor – the foyer, canteen, library and gym and all that – stuff gets moved around and changed all the time, usually overnight. That's when the technicians, like these two, crawl out of the

**55**

woodwork to make their little…adjustments."

Jonquil was shaking her head. Her cheeks puffed up while she pushed a deep breath through her mouth.

Cyan laughed. "It's part of the disorientation that keeps those memories away. You'll get used to it, much quicker than you think. Before you know it, it's the occasional day they leave things be that throws you."

"And what about that?" Jonquil nodded at one of the technicians, who was removing green clothes from a drawer and replacing them with red ones. "Let me guess: the uniform's colour changes every day too?"

"Exactly! You see? You're getting the hang of things already." Cyan grimaced at the closing drawer. "Shame it's red tomorrow. Probably my least—"

A bleeping from their pockets.

Cyan took out his locket and flicked it open.

Jonquil groaned. "Another shuffle?"

"No. Dinner time." Cyan grinned at her blanching face. "You hungry?"

# THE S WORD

By the time they reached the canteen, Jonquil looked perkier. She'd managed to unfasten herself from her bin and had left it on a technician's trolley somewhere in the upper rooms.

The canteen rung with noise – with the chatter and clatter of residents and cutlery. Jonquil had to raise her voice. "The walk did me some good. I always feel better after exercise."

"Super." Cyan was on the tips of his toes, eyeing the queue at the food counter. He scanned the rows of tables. "Aha! We're in luck. Looks like Teal and Ruby got the same dinner shift."

Jonquil slowed to survey the bustling space and the mosaics on the walls. "Those patterns – they're supposed to look like waves, right?" Her pupils rose. "And the lights on those ropes… They're sort of like…what you'd imagine on old ships."

"Don't get used to them. There'll be something else there tomorrow. We'd better queue before all the good grub's gone."

They'd soon filled their trays with macaroni cheese and rhubarb crumble. As they left the counter Cyan heard someone call his name. He turned and saw Dr Haven at a staff table, with Ms Ferryman and Professor Vadasz on either side of him. Dr Haven beckoned with a friendly flap of the hand.

As they headed over, Cyan spoke through the side of his mouth. "See that old guy next to Dr Haven? With the lab coat and don't-care hair? That's Professor Vadasz."

"Vadasz?" Jonquil squinted at the professor. "He doesn't look like a Vadasz. That sounds…I dunno, European? He looks like he's from East Asia or something."

"I don't think the staff here use their real names."

"Why not?"

"I'm not sure." Cyan slowed a little. "Never really thought about it." He frowned and picked up his pace. "Anyway, when we get to him, tell him how impressed you were by the *shuffle*. He always gets in a flap when residents call it that."

"Um." Jonquil seemed unsure. "I'm not sure I fancy upsetting him."

"He won't mind if *you* do it. You're new. Still learning."

Jonquil didn't look keen.

"You don't have to," whispered Cyan, smiling again now. "But it'd be a terrible waste."

When they reached the staff table, Dr Haven placed his knife and fork – in perfect symmetry – at each side of his steak, which had been sliced into neat, even segments. He dabbed his lips with a napkin. "Jonquil, how's your first day been?" His grey eyes lingered on her face, watching her expression.

Jonquil nodded meekly. "Good…I think. Cyan's been a great guide."

"Is that so?" The director raised a grey eyebrow at Cyan.

Cyan opened his mouth in exaggerated shock. "You sound surprised, Dr Haven."

Dr Haven smiled slyly. "You'll never surprise me, Cyan. Now, Jonquil, you've met Ms Ferryman…"

Ms Ferryman looked up from her meal, gave Jonquil a curt nod.

"Yes," replied Jonquil. "We've met."

"And what about the professor?"

The man on Dr Haven's other side shot up to clutch Jonquil's hand. His words were as brisk as his handshake. "Pleased to meet you, Jonquil. I'm Professor Vadasz. I look after the technical side of things here – the mechanisms, engineers, programmers and so on."

Cyan tapped Jonquil's ankle with his foot. She met his eyes briefly, swallowed subtly and returned the professor's smile. "I saw the…shuffle earlier. It's really something."

The professor froze. Every inch of him was still – apart from his eyelids, which fluttered for several seconds.

Cyan did his best to repress a smirk, but couldn't help cringing when Ms Ferryman shook her head at him.

The professor finally spoke. "*Shuffle*," he repeated, forcing the word between his lips.

He straightened up, puffing out his narrow chest. "Jonquil. The term we use here at the Elsewhere Sanctuary is reconfiguration. *Reconfiguration*." He drew out the word, labouring carefully over each syllable. "What takes place when the sanctuary reconfigures is as far from a…*shuffle* as anything can get. The term 'shuffle' suggests randomness, and I assure you, not a speck of chance is permitted in the process. It demands an incredibly *exact* science to have those rooms and walls rearrange in a way that not only avoids collision, but also allows the building to remain functional. A very advanced computer algorithm is required, which achieves the equivalent of traffic control in a city made of moving roads. Can you appreciate that, Jonquil?"

Jonquil stared at him momentarily, before blinking and nodding. "Yes, Professor."

Professor Vadasz's smile returned. "Then there'll be no more talk of shuffles."

Ms Ferryman cleared her throat. Her dark lips and forehead were creased in disapproval. "Cyan. I think you'd better take Jonquil to a table. You must both be hungry."

Cyan beamed and slapped his belly. "As a horse, Ms Ferryman. Sometime-somewhere!"

With a tap of his non-existent cap, he spun on his heels and guided Jonquil across the canteen to where Ruby and Teal were eating. "Ahoy! Mind if we join you?"

Ruby's freckles – dark against her tawny brown skin – gathered while she wrinkled her nose. "Hugely."

Cyan plopped his tray down, took a seat and gestured to Jonquil to do the same. "Jonquil, meet Teal and Ruby. Teal and Ruby, meet Jonquil."

"Ahoy, Jonquil," chorused the pair.

Cyan opened his mouth, hit by an urge to tell his friends what he'd seen at the whale bones – to ask Ruby and Teal what they made of it all. *Between green and red. S-7270.* But he caught himself and – glancing sourly at Dr Haven's table – realized how keen he was to get it off his chest. Somehow the bones were still bothering him.

*memory thieves*
*fight don't forget*

"So, Jonquil…" Teal straightened his wire spectacles with one hand, while using the other to point his fork at Jonquil. "We saw you talking to Professor Vadasz. You said the word, right?"

"Shuffle?"

Teal and Ruby froze and fluttered their eyelids in a parody of the professor, before giving in to giggles.

Cyan laughed along with them and felt a little better. He saw Jonquil smiling too, finally starting on her food.

Ruby swept a hand through her copper-brown curls. "How do you like the sanctuary, Jonquil?"

Jonquil chewed thoughtfully. "It's...a lot to take in. I mean, like, *a lot*."

"You'll settle in. It gets pretty blah." Without even a glance downwards, Ruby clutched the small cup of pills on her tray and tossed its contents into her mouth, before washing them down with some juice.

Cyan and Teal did the same with their own cups, then looked expectantly at Jonquil.

Jonquil's eyes moved to the pills – to their many shapes and pastel hues – in the paper cup on her tray. After nibbling her lower lip, she tipped them slowly into her mouth and gulped down some water.

Ruby shovelled cheesy pasta onto her fork. "Yeah, it's pretty chilled here. And there's loads of fun stuff to do." She popped the fork into her mouth and spoke around her food. "What did you make of the shuffle?"

Jonquil chewed slowly and swallowed. "It was...kind of intense."

"Just stay in your snug whenever it happens." Ruby's

eyes met Teal's and Cyan's. "Remember what happened to Moss…"

The boys nodded as one.

"Poor Moss," whispered Teal, giving a brisk shudder.

Jonquil cocked her head to one side. "Moss?"

Cyan wiped his mouth with the back of his hand. "Moss was one of the sanctuary's earliest residents. Supposedly fell out of his snug during a shuffle. Got mashed up between a moving wall and floor."

Jonquil's knife and fork clattered to her plate.

Ruby picked some macaroni from her teeth. "Rest in pieces, Moss."

"I'm not sure it's true, though," said Cyan. "Moss might be a myth. A bogeyman to keep residents in their snugs."

Teal was loosening his collar and scratching vigorously at his neck. "I think it really happened. Those rooms move about *way* too fast."

Cyan's fork met some burned, blackened pasta. He pushed it to the edge of his plate and hid it beneath a salad leaf.

"God, Teal!" It was Ruby. "Can you stop scratching yourself like that? You're putting me off my food."

"It's Cyan's fault. Boy racer here got sand all over me while he was skidding about on his quad."

Cyan began to smile.

"You nearly knocked me over! Do you even open your

eyes when you're riding those things?"

Cyan laughed. He could feel the pills from his paper cup taking effect. A tingling numbness spread from his forehead to the backs of his hands, and he found himself wondering why he'd been so worried about the whale bones. He smiled and rubbed his neck, enjoying the tingle on his scalp. Dr Haven was right. What he'd seen was just graffiti. Meaningless nonsense.

Teal was still fussing. "Even Fern drives better than you, and he's like…eight or something."

Cyan rolled his eyes and smiled at Jonquil. "One thing you'll quickly learn about Teal is that he *loves* to stress."

Teal's hands were in the air. "No I don't!"

"Yeah, you do. You're always looking for stuff to worry about. I asked Dr Haven about it once."

Teal crossed his arms. "I bet you didn't."

"I did."

Teal's arms began to unknot. "Seriously?" He leaned towards Cyan, his eyes growing large behind his glasses. "What did he say?"

"It's just a tendency in your character. He said it shouldn't be any cause for concern."

Teal's chin dropped. *"Shouldn't?* What's he mean?"

"Well, I can't remember his exact words." Cyan saw the panic mounting in Teal's eyes. "Actually, I'm pretty sure he said it's *not* a cause for concern."

"No, you said *shouldn't*! And shouldn't means 'might', right? It means there's a chance my worrying'll lead to something that…that *is* a cause for concern. What if…" His words trailed off and he stared at his plate.

Ruby hooted and thumped him playfully on the arm. "I can't believe it, Teal. You're actually worrying about worrying. That's amazing, even for you."

Teal straightened on his chair. "Yeah? Well if it's amazing to care about stuff – unlike *some* people around here –" he eyed Cyan meaningfully – "then yeah, I'm amazing."

Ruby patted his forearm where she'd hit him, then drummed Jonquil's hand with the butt of her knife. "So, Jonquil, how far away is the sea?"

"How far?"

Ruby was bobbing on her seat. "Yeah. Did you get an idea from your helicopter ride?"

"I couldn't tell. The pilot put a blindfold on me before we took off. But the sea can't be far, right? I saw the harbour outside. And the lighthouse."

"Sure," said Ruby. "The lighthouse is boarded up, though. And you can't see the sea, even from high up on the helipad."

Jonquil gave this some thought. "Oh. That's true, I guess. I figured the tide was out?"

"Bit far for the tide to go out, isn't it?"

Cyan pushed some salad around his plate. "The tide

never comes in, Jonquil. It went out and never came back."

Jonquil's brow crumpled. She scratched the long bridge of her nose. "How's that possible?"

Cyan shrugged. "Dunno. I overheard some staff talking about it once. Could be industrial irrigation. Or chemicals and pollution, but they weren't sure. They're as clueless as we are about where the island is or why the sea's receded. But yeah, the tide's gone for good. I can't remember the last time I saw the sea. None of us can. And we go pretty far out on the sands."

Jonquil's knife and fork were still on her plate. Her mouth hung open for some moments. "So even the staff don't know where we are? Or where this island actually *is*?"

"Well, I guess the helicopter pilot must have some bearings. And the hovercraft pilots too. But Ms Ferryman told me new staff wear blindfolds when they're flown in. Dr Haven's pretty thorough in keeping us cut off from things. It's for our own good."

"Cut off," murmured Jonquil. "And the rest of the world…" Her gaze fell to her hands. "Our old lives…"

"That's why you came here, right? To get away and forget?" Cyan frowned. "Hey. You okay?"

He leaned a little closer to Jonquil. Teal and Ruby did the same, and all three of them gawped at the tears welling in her eyes.

Jonquil edged away, scowling and wiping her face. "Stop it! It's rude to stare, you know!"

The trio withdrew. Teal cringed. "Sorry, Jonquil. It's just... I can't remember the last time I saw someone cry."

Ruby's hazel eyes were wide. "Yeah, what's it like?"

Jonquil's anger evaporated. "What's it like?" She looked confused. "You mean, to cry?"

All three of them nodded keenly.

Jonquil's lips tried to form words. She put a hand against her forehead. "I...don't know. It's like—" She shook her head. "It hurts, sort of. But not properly. Kind of an ache. It's like...letting something out."

The trio pondered this in silence. Cyan rubbed his chin. A smile tugged the edges of his mouth. "So it's like...a painful number two?"

"No!" Jonquil screwed up her face. "That's gross."

Cyan stopped snickering when Ruby thumped his arm so hard he nearly fell from his seat. "Ignore Cyan, Jonquil. He's an idiot and he suffers from delusions of humour."

Cyan rubbed his arm. "Hey! You laugh at me all the time."

"Yeah: *at.*" Ruby addressed Jonquil. "Anyway, you'll soon forget how to cry as well. In the meantime, I'd say you need some cheering up. Tomorrow we'll take you to the Serenity."

"What's the Serenity?" asked Jonquil.

"A lot of fun. You'll see."

Cyan drummed his palms against the table, before tapping Teal's hand and pointing at his tray. "You owe me your pudding."

One of Teal's eyebrows rose. "What are you on about?"

"Don't play dumb. You lost our bet." Cyan wagged his thumb in Jonquil's direction. "Today's helicopter delivery *was* a new resident. I was right; you were wrong. So come on. Hand it over."

Teal spluttered and squirmed on his seat. "But it's rhubarb crumble! Can't you wait 'til tomorrow? You know it's my favourite."

"And rightly so. It's the king of crumbles. The duke of desserts. That's why it's my favourite too. Send it this way."

Grimacing sullenly, Teal slid his bowl across the table to Cyan, who began tucking in straight away.

"If it helps," said Cyan, beaming through his food, "you've earned yourself a substitute dessert."

"Yeah?"

"Humble pie."

Teal shook his head with a sigh. "Your jokes are as bad as your driving."

Cyan started his second rhubarb crumble, then paused to point at Jonquil with a custard-covered spoon. "Are you all right? You're doing that thing with your fingers again."

Jonquil sat on her hands.

"We'll show you the games room and lounge tonight. That'll cheer you up. And if that fails, there's the Serenity tomorrow. The Serenity's *always* a blast."

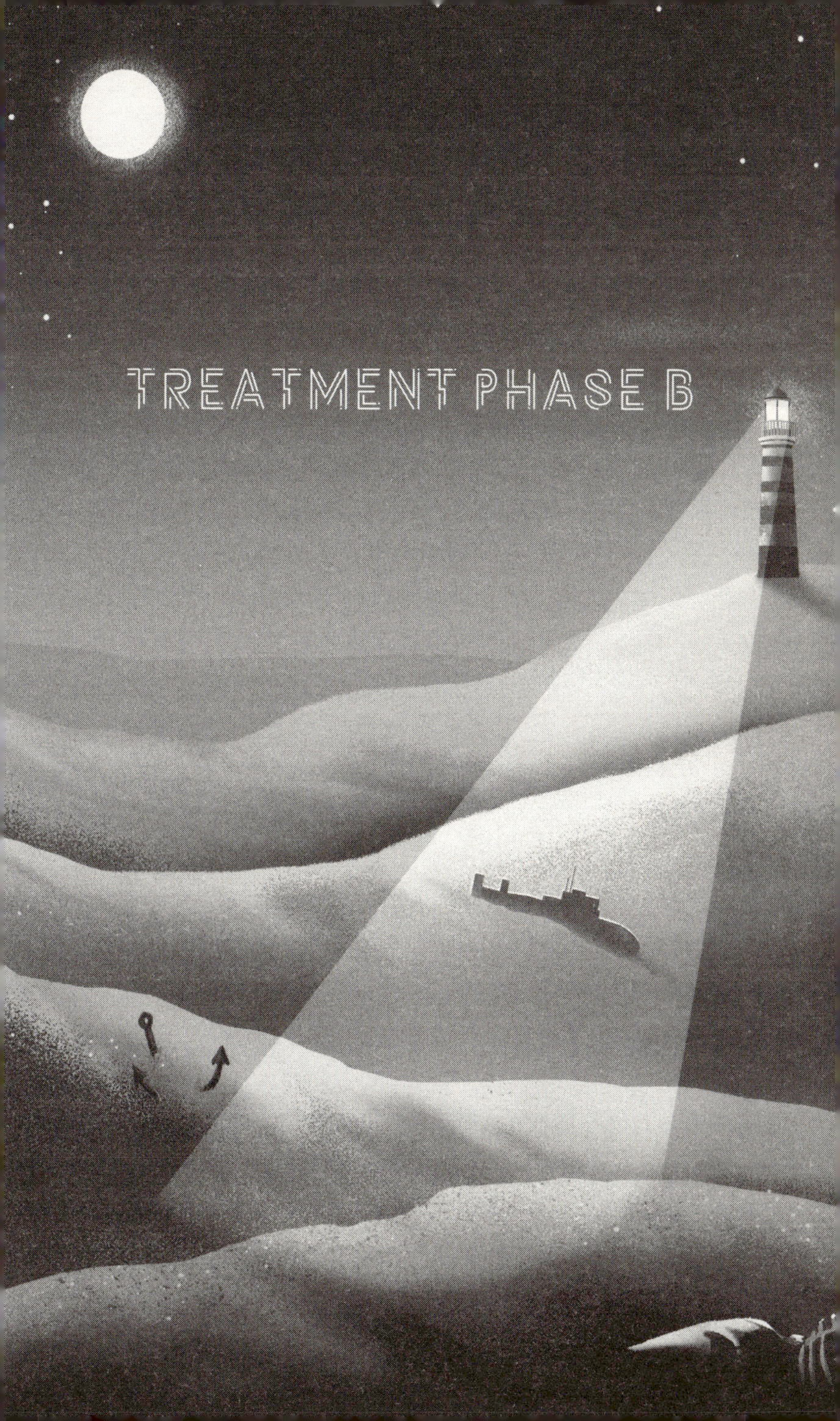
TREATMENT PHASE B

# GET SET

The next morning Cyan wolfed down breakfast, threw a packed lunch into his satchel, then dashed from the canteen to the foyer. He was heading for the sanctuary's exit when a beep sent his hand to his pocket. He pulled out his locket and flipped it open.

*Dr Haven's office. ASAP.*

Cyan sighed and was soon knocking on the director's door. He pushed it open as it buzzed.

"You wanted to see me, Doctor?"

Dr Haven glanced up from some paperwork on his desk, stood and beckoned Cyan in. "I did."

Before Cyan could even sit down, the director handed him some pills and a glass of water. He walked immediately away and tugged the curtain in the corner aside.

Cyan downed his pills and nodded at the strobe chair. "Strobe therapy today?"

73

Smiling wryly, the doctor tapped the chair's console. "As perceptive as ever, Cyan."

Cyan shrugged and crossed the office. While stretching across the chair he was struck by a thought. "Doctor?"

"Mm-hm."

"Is this anything to do with…what I saw yesterday?" He drummed his hands against the leather. "You know, on the bones?"

The director chuckled. "That's an odd thing to ask, Cyan. You know very well we can only touch memories from before residents arrive here. We have an ethical—"

"Code. Right. Of course." Cyan gave an embarrassed laugh. "Sorry, wasn't thinking." He shrugged. "Just feels like a while since my last strobe session. Thought this one might be something to do with the whale bones. Since it's happening so soon after." He felt a chill as Dr Haven attached pads to his temples.

The doctor tutted playfully. "A little thing called coincidence. I'm sure you've heard of it." He cracked his knuckles. "But now that you bring it up, you'll remember from our conversation that you weren't to talk of what you saw at the bones. It might be best if you started putting that into practice."

"Even with you?"

"Even with me. Have you mentioned it to anyone?"

Cyan's eyes followed the chair's concave screen, which

Dr Haven positioned close to his face. "No. No one."

"Good. You'll no doubt remember what I said about consequences."

Cyan turned his head to the director. "Yeah. But what—"

"Eyes on the screen, Cyan."

The chair began to hum. Its steady vibration was soft, soothing. Whirring sounds stretched and echoed in Cyan's ears.

The doctor's voice seemed to reach him from a distance. "So tell me: what do you have planned today?"

Cyan had to concentrate to answer. "We're going to the Serenity." The words were slow and sticky in his mouth. "Showing Jonquil."

"Excellent," replied Dr Haven. "I'm sure she'll benefit immensely from explorrrrrriiinngg ttthhhhheeee…"

The doctor's words merged into a flat, murmuring drone. Cyan's breathing slowed, and all the world was white, flashing light.

A little later, Cyan found himself blinking at clouds. He was standing on the marble stairway outside the sanctuary.

Teal and Jonquil were already perched on the steps, with Ruby pacing back and forth below.

Cyan saluted and hollered. "Ahoy! Everyone ready?"

While heading down the steps he pulled a face and flapped his blazer. "Red uniforms today – my least favourite. I look like an overgrown raspberry."

Jonquil was twirling long black hair between her fingers. "I think it looks good on you." She flushed suddenly and began staring at her plimsolls.

"Nah. Doesn't suit me."

Ruby nodded in earnest. "I agree. You look vile."

Teal sighed. "All the colours look bad on me. And these shirts…" He scratched the soft brown skin at the nape of his neck. "They're always so prickly."

Cyan aimed a thumb across the harbour towards the hangar. "Come on. Better grab quads quick, before Teal gets started on itchy shirts again."

Teal cocked his head at him. "Just try not to crash into anyone, yeah?"

They were soon goggled up and rolling out of the hangar on three quads, with Jonquil sharing Cyan's. "Sure you don't want your own bike?" he asked. "Last chance."

"Not just yet."

"Your call. Just make sure you hold on tight. These things are fast."

Cyan and Ruby led the way down the cobbled ramp to the sand, with Teal following behind. They passed some younger residents who were digging happily not far from the bank, using buckets, spades and shells to build sprawling sand sculptures. The children waved as they rolled by, and after an exchange of cheery ahoys, Cyan revved his engine and the quads picked up speed.

A sudden low humming had Cyan peering sideways. He smiled and slowed his quad.

Ruby decelerated too. "What's keeping you, slow coach?"

"Guess who's come out to play."

Twisting to look backwards, Cyan saw the hovercraft crawling down the harbour's ramp. The younger residents turned tail from the mammoth machine, their blazers flapping in the blast from its immense twin propellers. The craft hit the sand and started to accelerate.

Ruby and Teal watched the hovercraft draw nearer. Cyan hollered over the growing noise. "We've got a head start! On your marks, get set—"

Ruby sped ahead with brown curls thrashing. Cyan twisted his throttle as far as it would go, and heard Jonquil yelp when the quad jerked forward, her arms tightening around his stomach.

With Ruby at the fore and Teal racing beside Cyan, the three quads zoomed through the space between the stone piers' tips. They bounced and hurtled across the dunes, their engines buzzing in ear-piercing unison, but Cyan could still hear the hovercraft gaining on them, like a sandstorm on their tails.

He felt it before he saw it – a deep, humming throb that charged and rippled the air. Jonquil squealed when the hovercraft's black air-cushion drew up beside them.

The squall of turbines and propellers filled Cyan's ears. Sand hissed against his goggles while he peered sidelong to watch the hovercraft match the quads' pace. He could see several shipping containers on the loading area along its centre, and two pilots in its raised orange cockpit, who waved through busy windscreen wipers before the hovercraft sped away, increasing its distance from the quads.

The noise died down, giving way to Ruby's whooping. Cyan grinned at her, then noticed faint noises from Jonquil, who was pushing her face into his back.

"You okay?" he asked.

She lifted her face and he could hear that she was laughing. "Yeah! That was…was…"

"I know, right?" Cyan laughed too, then waved an arm at Ruby and Teal. At his signal, all three quads turned east. The sanctuary's cove shrank behind them, and Cyan felt the ground steepening subtly. They were heading deeper into what used to be sea.

Jonquil was quiet for some time, until she leaned to Cyan's ear. "I can't believe this place. The sand – it's everywhere."

"Yup."

"And we just went past some… I think they were… whale bones?"

Whale bones…

Cyan peered over his shoulder at the curving ribs, and found himself thinking inexplicably of colours. Not just any colours, though. Two in particular – as random as they were vivid. Red and green. Green and red.

Something else came to mind. The letter S. And some numbers. Seven, two…seven, zero?

Cyan's eyes narrowed behind his goggles. Where had these thoughts come from? And why were they triggered by the whale bones? They had nothing to do with them. Or with anything else, for that matter. The bones were boring. A quiet spot for reading, nothing more.

Maybe that was it. Maybe he'd read some books there – books that mentioned those colours and numbers.

It was strange, though. He felt like there was something more. Something fuzzy and vague, niggling at the fringes of his memory. Something that had been bothering him…

Cyan scrunched his eyes shut briefly, trying to figure out what he was trying to remember. But all that came was a blank, flashing whiteness.

The quad hit a bump and he opened his eyes. He heard Jonquil speak.

"Is that what they are, then? Actual whale bones?"

Cyan nodded. "Yeah. There's a few about."

"And those too?" Jonquil pointed ahead at a corroded ship, which looked like it had ploughed headfirst into a dune.

"Plenty."

Jonquil stared at the sandscape. "So it's true, then. The sea isn't coming back."

"Looks that way."

Jonquil fell silent. She wiped her goggles before she spoke again. "It's so salty here. I can taste it in the air."

Cyan looked up to see swirls of thinning cloud. "You get used to it. And the salt has its perks."

"Perks?"

"Just wait."

They continued to ride, following the grooves between dunes and dodging tracts of beach grass.

Cyan looked up again. "Here it comes."

Clouds gave way to sunbeams. Bleached bones and rusty hulls began to glitter. Cyan heard a small gasp.

Ruby glanced backwards and must have noticed Jonquil's expression. She slowed to pull closer and shouted across the air. "It's called salt-sparkle!"

Jonquil nodded. She pointed at a towering bluff of rock towards the east. "Why are there, like, hills here? Didn't this used to be sea?" Horizontal grooves lined the bluff's yellow stone, which glimmered with salt in the brightening light.

"Not hills; they used to be islands! Good caves in that one – awesome view from the top! We'll take you some time, but today's all about the Serenity."

"What *is* the Serenity?"

Ruby pointed ahead. Something colossal and white was jutting from the ground, like a vast column aimed at the sun. Cyan glanced backwards and laughed at Jonquil's dropping chin.

As they drew nearer, the immense size of the *Serenity*'s tilted hull hit home. Cyan had seen it many times, but couldn't help the appreciative whistle that trilled between his teeth.

He turned to look at Jonquil, who was taking in the sight of the giant cruise ship. Its rear protruded at an angle from a deep chasm of rock, and its long belly was red with rust, with its steel crumpled and torn where it met the chasm's edge.

"*That*," he said, "is the *Serenity*." He pointed at the cruise ship's full name – *Regal Serenity* – written in faded blue on the hull's side.

The three quads pulled up by the brink of the rift. After removing their goggles and shaking sand from their hair, the four residents stared deep into the shadows. Far below, the *Serenity*'s nose sat crushed against the chasm's base.

Cyan saw Jonquil's next question coming, so he waved a hand at the sandy abyss. "Used to be a deeper patch of sea."

Ruby clambered down the chasm's lip. "Come on, then. Let's get in."

Jonquil gaped at her. "Get in?"

Teal touched her elbow. He pointed at a wide gash in the keel, a little way down the chasm's slope.

Jonquil began to wring her hands. "Oh."

# THE SERENITY

They were soon on the ship and heading up three decks of engine rooms, past long runs of generators, pistons, pipes and flaking machinery. When they emerged from the lower decks, the dank stench of rust left Cyan's nostrils. In its place hung the must of rotting cabins.

They were trekking through a mildewed, carpeted corridor when a door number caught his eye: *7284.*

With the others still walking, Cyan paused and studied the brass numbers. He thought back to what had come to him on the quad.

*S-7270*

Could the S stand for *Serenity*?

Teal, Ruby and Jonquil were further up the corridor's slope. Jonquil asked something. Cyan could just make out Ruby's reply.

"…never found anyone. I guess the passengers all got

rescued before the ship went down. Cyan pretended to be a body on the toilet once, though. Really freaked Teal out."

A scoff from Teal. "So what? I got him back."

Ruby hooted, tapping Jonquil's arm. "Yeah, he jumped out from a wardrobe in one of the cabins. Cyan thought it was a zombie attack or something."

"Almost needed a change of trousers," snorted Teal. He forced a strained laugh and rubbed his neck. "That mouldy wardrobe gave me a mean rash, though."

Cyan smiled to himself. Another of Teal's imaginary rashes.

Backtracking down the corridor, he counted the doors and stopped when he reached his destination.

Cabin 7270.

The door was open. Cyan entered.

It was one of the *Serenity*'s more luxurious cabins. A wide plump bed was banked against the wall, its mattress as mouldy as the drapes that hung askew by the window. A widescreen TV dangled from a bracket on the wall, and the once-lavish furnishings were splintered and rotten, mildewed and bloated.

Cyan gazed at the chasm's distant wall, which he could see through the cabin's speckled window. And then, after pushing his glasses up the bridge of his nose, he began to search the wardrobes and drawers for anything unusual.

He found just mounds of fuzz that used to be clothes.

Gowns and dresses speckled black, white and green. Phone chargers, tarnished jewellery and rotten high heels.

He moved quickly on to the bedside tables. The first one was empty. The second one was empty too, except…

Except it wasn't. Not quite. Something had been scratched into the drawer's wooden base. Lines of tiny writing, careful and deep.

Cyan read the first line – *between green and red* – and his hand went to his chest.

Green and red; the colours that had come to him on the quad, when he'd looked at the whale bones. Just like the numbers that had brought him to this cabin: 7270.

Faint memories were beginning to stir.

Taking a deep breath, Cyan got to his knees and read on:

*Me: Ruth McMurphy*
*Mum: Helen McMurphy, blonde pixie hair, blue-grey eyes, best cuddles ever, smells like fresh soil in the garden, sings quietly in the bath*
*Dad: James McMurphy, bald shiny head, nerdy glasses, tickly black beard, brown eyes, Santa belly laugh, terrible jokes, smells like baking*
*Brother: Ben McMurphy, scoundrel, long blond curls, massive blue eyes, cute nose, noisy and lovely and smells like malty milk*

*Home: Nottingham in England, by the horse field in*
*Bestwood*
*Best to deceive the memory thieves*
*Fight don't forget, hold on or it's gone*

Cyan's mouth was dry. His stirring memories settled, sharpened into shape by those final lines.

It all came back to him. He'd seen words like these before. Carved into a whale's rib.

*best to deceive the memory thieves*
*between green and red, fight don't forget*

But why had he forgotten? Why couldn't he remember on the quad?

Cyan cast his mind back to before he'd hit the dunes with Jonquil and the others. He remembered rushing his breakfast, heading through the foyer. Then being called to Dr Haven's office, sitting on the strobe chair…

That was *it*. It was the only explanation. Dr Haven had weakened Cyan's memory of what he'd found on the bones – a memory that must have lingered somewhere at the back of his mind, faint and fading but still there. Still there enough, at least, to be roused by the message in this drawer and the numbers that had led him here: colours and numbers he hadn't mentioned to the doctor.

Cyan bit his lip. Dr Haven had broken the sanctuary's ethical code; he'd tampered with recent memories. And on top of that he'd lied. He'd told Cyan the strobe session had nothing to do with the whale bones – that its timing was pure chance.

*memory thieves*

Dr Haven said the bone words were nonsense. But if they were nonsense, why go to the trouble of erasing them? And hadn't the doctor thieved after all?

Cyan peered again into the drawer. He felt his palms growing hot while he reread the words.

What *was* all this? Why the bone code and this hidden note? It seemed that someone – this Ruth McMurphy – was secretly trying to keep memories of her old life. But that was another thing that confused him. Why would anyone want to keep their old memories? People came to the sanctuary to forget; to escape whatever terrible things had happened to them. Cyan had played the clip on his locket enough times – had seen himself cry and beg for help – to know that much was true.

Cyan's hands were shaking. But not from the fact that Dr Haven had lied to him. It was something else. Something he still couldn't put his finger on, but which made his stomach cramp and squirm.

Footsteps. In the corridor.

Instinctively, Cyan shot to his feet and slammed the drawer shut.

Ruby's head popped through the doorway. She knitted

her brow and entered, with Teal and Jonquil just behind. "Hey. Where'd you disappear to?"

Cyan was about to tell his friends what he'd found, but he caught himself and bit his tongue. He thought back to what Dr Haven had said, about what would happen if Cyan mentioned anything to anyone. About consequences.

What exactly were those consequences? And were they just for Cyan, or for the people he told?

He swallowed and mimicked Ruby's frown. "Me? Where'd *you* disappear to? I saw something through the window and said we should check it out. Didn't you guys hear?"

"Obviously not. What did you see?"

While everyone looked through the window, Cyan glanced at the bedside table. His throat felt tight and coarse. "Nothing, I guess. Must have imagined it."

"Pfft." Ruby turned from the window. "You're being weird. Even by your standards."

"Cyan?" It was Jonquil. She looked concerned. "Your face is all flushed. Are you okay?"

Cyan wiped his forehead, felt hot sweat on the back of his hand. "Shipshape. It's just a bit…toasty in here, right?"

"Hardly." Ruby was exploring the cabin's large, stately dressing table. She picked up some lipstick, which must have rolled along the sloping table before stopping against a stained, battered make-up box.

Teal joined her and screwed up his face. "You're not actually going to use that, are you? It'll probably make you ill."

Ruby pulled off the lipstick's silver lid and studied its contents. "Probably would. It's not for my face, though…"

Grinning all the while, Ruby used the lipstick to trace her reflection on the dressing table's wide mirror, with dots for freckles and long squiggles for hair. She passed the lipstick to Teal, who shrugged and traced his own reflection. It had a little less height than Ruby's and a broader face, with oval spectacles and a short, rounded afro.

Jonquil was next, tracing her face and long, centre-parted hair. She handed the lipstick to Cyan. Glad for the distraction, he added his own outline, finishing with his floppy fringe and chunky glasses.

Four doodle-friends smiled outwards from the mirror. But Cyan needed more distraction.

"A masterpiece!" He clapped his hands, almost wincing at the cheer he'd forced into his voice. "Are we done? Let's show Jonquil why we're really here."

They left cabin 7270 and continued on their way.

Jonquil moved slowly at first, clambering against the slant of the decks. But by the time they reached the decrepit lobbies she was in her element. She threw herself up staircases steepened by the hull's tilt and soon took the lead, so that the others had to shout directions from behind. Flushed and grinning, she vaulted over the chairs, luggage and debris that had fallen prey to gravity and piled up around doorways and mezzanines.

"She's fast," panted Ruby.

Cyan skirted a fallen chandelier, which gleamed like a mound of jewels on the mouldy carpet. "Tell me about it."

Eventually the trio staggered through a steel door and into fresh air. They found Jonquil gripping a rail not far from the door, staring down the slope of the cruise ship's top deck.

Cyan joined her and followed her gaze. Loungers, deck chairs and drifts of sand were piled against rusting walls, battered terraces and ghostly cocktail bars. At least three empty swimming pools pitted the deck, before it reached the ship's nose at the base of the chasm.

Jonquil looked at him with her mouth hanging open. She seemed unable to speak.

"Yup," agreed Cyan.

Jonquil's gaze returned to the slope. "So what now?"

Cyan shuffled to the deck's edge, where rows of plastic drums were fixed to steel brackets. Ruby was pulling a long cord from one of the barrels.

"We go to the bottom," he replied.

"What? We've just climbed to the top!"

"Yep. So we can get back down."

"Then why not go down through the decks?"

Cyan smiled at the thought of what was coming. He felt a flutter of excitement rise from his stomach, cutting through the thoughts that had followed him from the cabin. "Some things, Jonquil, are more about the journey than the destination."

He found the cord attached to another plastic drum and unwound it until he felt it jar. With his eyes meeting Ruby's, they yanked their cords and leaped back as one. Both drums popped open, and there was a steady hiss while their contents unfolded and expanded.

Cyan pointed at the two inflated life rafts, each one bright orange and big enough for four. "This is how we get down."

Jonquil rubbed her forehead. "Lifeboats? I don't get it. There's no water."

"No, but they'll protect us –" Cyan kicked his life raft's inflated base – "while we shoot down the biggest slide in the world." He tipped his head towards the sloping deck, then took two oars from inside the raft's orange canopy. "We'll need one of these each, so we can steer away from any…bumps. Come on. Hop in."

"You've got to be joking."

"Do we look like we're joking?"

Ruby and Teal had already dragged their own raft to the centre of the deck and climbed in. They leaned out from the opening in the canopy's front, so that their oars protruded at each side.

Ruby grinned. Her curls were fiery in the light that pierced the canopy. "It's safe, Jonquil." She held a hand to Teal's mouth before he could say otherwise. "We've done it a million times before and we're all still here, aren't we? So hop in. You won't regret it."

Jonquil looked at Cyan, who'd dragged his raft next to Ruby's and clambered in. He held an oar out to her. "You were pretty fast coming up here. You think you're as fast going down?"

Jonquil's eyes narrowed. Cocking her head and smiling slightly, she grasped the oar and got in next to Cyan.

"Super. All hands on deck." Anticipation was still bubbling in Cyan's belly, but not with its usual keenness. Silently, he cursed the whale bones and drawers, and did his best to push all thoughts of them aside.

"Last ones to the bottom are rotten eggs." He craned his neck to Ruby and Teal. "In fact, they're the flies that eat the rotten eggs. Or actually: the bacteria that live on the flies that eat the—"

"We get the idea." Ruby was jerking on her knees to shunt her raft along the slope. Teal grumbled but jerked in sync, so that the raft gathered momentum and started slipping down the deck.

Cyan shot an imaginary starter gun into the air – "BANG!" – and began lurching with Jonquil, until their raft was moving on its own. They'd gained enough speed to make its canopy flutter when Cyan clocked some jacuzzi steps on collision course ahead.

"Jonquil!" he shouted, but there was no need. She slammed her oar against a passing wall so that their raft skidded left, just enough to miss the stained jacuzzi.

Cyan beamed at Jonquil, who grinned back and laughed. But the moment's distraction cost them; the raft clipped some awning and spun to send them speeding down backwards.

Cyan cackled at the sight of the ship's raised, dwindling rear; heard the joyful clatter of loungers knocked aside by the raft. His worries disappeared. There was only the race now. Only the adrenaline and the wind and the hurtling deck.

As one, Jonquil and Cyan barged their oars against the floor; by the time they'd revolved they were bouncing across an astroturf putting green. While golf flags whipped and lashed the canopy, Cyan saw Ruby and Teal's raft some way ahead, narrowly dodging a cocktail bar and scattering aluminium chairs and tables.

"They're too far ahead!" shouted Jonquil. "We can't catch up!"

Cyan wriggled his eyebrows. "Not unless they mess up." He hollered as loudly as he could. "*Watch out!* Ruby! Teal! On your right! Stairs going down! Hard to see!"

There was no stairway, but the pair must have believed

him. He heard a frenzied thumping of oars and the raft drifted left. Cyan whooped when it bounced off a hot tub and spun towards a gaping swimming pool. His own raft caught up while the other one spiralled, and he saw Ruby and Teal plunge out of sight. There was a rubbery thump, followed by a puff of sand and a howl of rage from Ruby.

Cyan and Jonquil were both laughing so hard that their eyes watered. With the aid of some frenetic oar-work, they dodged the pool and closed in on the mattresses stacked against the ship's bow. Cyan threw down his oar, struggling to stay upright while he opened his arms to Jonquil. "Hold on tight – brace for impact!"

Jonquil tossed her oar aside and they clutched each other just as the raft crashed, sending them tumbling across mattresses and old life rafts. The canopy was a blur of orange rubber, above them one moment and below them the next. By the time the raft came to a stop it was alive with hysterical laughter.

It took some time for the laughter to die away. Cyan and Jonquil lay still in the orange light, waiting for the dizziness to pass.

Jonquil's breathing gradually slowed. She broke the silence. "Ruby was right."

Cyan pulled himself up. "About what?"

"I don't regret it."

It took a while for Cyan to get his bearings and find the

raft's exit. "Quite a rush, isn't it?" He stuck his head through the opening. Outside, the chasm's base was immense and dark with depth.

Jonquil shifted behind him. "Talking of Ruby... What's the deal between you two?"

"Deal?" Cyan glanced back to see Jonquil winding some hair around her finger.

"Yeah. Are you like...boyfriend and girlfriend or something?"

Cyan's laugh echoed along the chasm. "No way. No way at all."

"Oh."

Jonquil looked thoughtful in a way that confused Cyan. He scratched the tip of his nose. "The sanctuary doesn't have stuff like that."

"Really?"

Cyan frowned and pinched his bottom lip. "Never really thought about it, but it's true. It's just the way things are, I guess." He snorted a gentle laugh through his nose. "Just the idea of it seems funny, you know? Kind of weird."

"Weird..." repeated Jonquil. Her dark eyes flickered downwards.

Cyan began to feel uncomfortable, although he couldn't fathom why.

He cleared his throat. "Come on. Let's get out of this thing."

# DISCLOSURE

Cyan and Jonquil took the sandwiches from their packed lunches and munched in silence. They were on the chasm's sandy base, perched on some dining chairs pilfered from the *Serenity*.

It wasn't long before the second raft hit the ship's bow.

When Teal and Ruby reached them, Ruby gave Cyan's shoulder a wallop.

"There wasn't a stairwell," she grumbled. "I checked, after we spent ages dragging our raft out of that pool. You cheated."

Teal took a seat. Cyan straightened his glasses. "All's fair in love and…races down giant shipwrecks."

"No, it's not." Ruby's scowl sent dark freckles gathering around her nose. She kicked a rusty basket at the centre of the ring of chairs, then began filling it with wood from a mound of broken furniture. "I see you didn't get the fire going. You know the first one down's supposed to do it. And yet you never do."

"Um…" All moisture left Cyan's mouth. He pushed his chair further back from the metal basket, and watched uneasily while Ruby used a lighter and some rolled-up menus to get the fire started.

Flames were soon rising. Cyan kept his eyes off the fire, but could feel its heat against his hands and face. His shoulders tensed with every pop from the crackling wood and he took deep, discreet breaths to steady his heartbeat.

What was left of his sandwich sat untouched on his lap. The smoke had killed his appetite and his throat was too dry to swallow. But he noticed Jonquil peering at him, so he put the bread back to his mouth, doing his best to hide his unease.

The four friends sat in silence, until Jonquil used her toe to nudge a fish skeleton half-buried in sand. "Animals," she sighed.

"Hm?" Cyan eyed what remained of the fish.

Jonquil tipped her head back and gazed at the grey sky framed by the chasm's mouth. "It took me a while to figure it out – what's missing. There're no animals on the island. Not even birds. The sky's always so quiet. I haven't seen a single creature since I got here."

Teal's lips curled into a playful smile. "There used to be loads. 'Til Cyan scared them all off with his driving."

Cyan's eyes were rolling. "Hardy har." He looked at Jonquil. "Ignore him. There's never been animals here."

"But isn't that weird?" asked Jonquil. "To have no animals around? Not even bugs or something? All I've seen here is bones and shells." Her forehead creased. "There's something sort of…dead about this place. Don't you think?"

Cyan frowned at the frail, crystallized skeleton. "Probably something to do with the sea being gone. You know, ecosystems and all that."

Teal nodded thoughtfully. "Yeah. That's probably it."

Jonquil didn't look convinced. "No. Ecosystems exist anywhere. Life always finds a way. But not here. Here on the island there's just… There's just us."

Cyan was struggling to tear his gaze from the dead fish's eye socket. Each crackle from the fire sent him deeper into its darkness, and he found himself thinking again about the message in cabin 7270.

A sniff from Jonquil. "Guys," she began. "I can call you friends now, right?"

"Sure," said Ruby. Teal and Cyan nodded.

"In that case…"

Cyan managed to look up. Jonquil was kneading her knuckles. Her voice dropped to a whisper. "I know it's not allowed, but I was wondering whether you guys would mind if…if perhaps I talk about what happened to me. You know. Before I came here."

Three pairs of eyes widened. Teal tensed, pushing himself into his chair's backrest.

"No." Ruby's voice was firm. "Sorry, Jonquil. You know we can't do that."

Jonquil shrugged meekly. "I know. But—"

"You're not allowed to talk about your past," interrupted Cyan. "No one is. It'll compromise your treatment. You might even compromise *our* treatment."

"But no one has to know," insisted Jonquil. Tears were gathering on her eyelids. "I just feel like…like I need to let some of it out. There are things I need to say." Her voice thickened. "Things I need to share…"

Cyan threw his palms up. "Don't do this, Jonquil." His heart was racing again. He'd never been in this situation before; no one had ever tried to talk about their past. But he knew the rules. He'd have to alert the sanctuary if Jonquil kept going. And he wasn't allowed to listen.

The legs of Ruby's chair scraped backwards through the sand. Teal had a hand on the side of his seat and was raising himself from its base. Sweat glistened on his forehead. His chest began to quake with panicked breaths. "The rules…" he croaked.

Jonquil saw them all shifting. A tear rolled down her cheek. "Please listen," she croaked. "It happened months ago, just after Diwali. My mum was—"

Teal was the first to flee. Jonquil stopped when Cyan

and Ruby followed suit, knocking back their chairs and sprinting in separate directions.

Cyan made a dash for the *Serenity*. He glanced over his shoulder, saw Ruby and Teal running for a rocky mound.

Jonquil was alone by the fallen chairs, revolving on her feet to watch the trio scarper. "Come back!" she wailed. "Pleeeeease!"

But the three of them kept running.

Cyan crouched in the shadow of the *Serenity*'s keel. He peered around its edge to see Jonquil staggering back and forth, unsure which direction to run in.

"Mum was driving us home!" she screamed. "Me and my sister! My beautiful little sister…" She fell to her knees but continued to wail. "Mum was in a bad mood 'cos we'd—"

Cyan threw his palms over his ears but could still hear Jonquil's dull screeching. He pushed an ear against his shoulder and used his free hand to yank his locket from his trousers. After thumbing it open and pressing its screen, he held it to his mouth and panted, "*Disclosure! It's Jonquil! Disclosure!*"

He made out a few words that flew from Jonquil's direction – something about an argument – and thrust the locket into his pocket before slamming his palm back against his ear.

Cyan wasn't sure how long he'd been waiting before swells of wind began racing along the chasm. The air pulsed and howled, and he peeked around the keel to see Jonquil standing rigid with her back to him, her long hair flailing in the gale. Up above, the sanctuary's helicopter appeared at the chasm's mouth.

Its steady descent whipped up a storm of salt and sand. Cyan could only just make out Mr Banter as the helicopter's side door opened.

Jonquil backed away through miniature cyclones. Mr Banter stepped out casually, brandishing something in his hand. Cyan squinted through whorls of yellow and white. It was some sort of cartridge; rectangular, plastic and pale.

Mr Banter aimed the cartridge at Jonquil and a long needle sprang from its top. Its thin metal winked in the helicopter's lights.

Jonquil screamed and turned, but Mr Banter was too quick. He leaped forward and smothered her head in his giant forearm.

A surge of sickness hit Cyan's stomach. The violence of Mr Banter's grip sent him out from cover, and as he ran to Jonquil he saw her eyes – wide and white with terror and betrayal – fall upon him.

He continued to run with his arm stretched towards her, and cried out when Mr Banter plunged the needle into her neck.

The screaming stopped. Jonquil stiffened, then dropped to hang limply from Mr Banter's arm. He dragged her into the helicopter and slammed the door shut before it rose through sand and shadows.

Cyan fell to his hands and knees. His chest heaved and his ribs felt brittle against his hammering heart.

With the helicopter tilting and soaring above them, Teal and Ruby emerged to join him. Ruby's face was rigid with shock. Teal watched the helicopter's tail disappear. He hugged himself tightly, trembling with emotion.

The drone of rotor blades faded, leaving only empty sky.

# GREY OCEANS

Cyan was soon on the psychiatrist's couch in Dr Haven's office. He'd been summoned by a bleep from his locket. It came as no surprise.

Cyan fidgeted on the creaking brown leather, glaring at the butterflies that covered the far wall. He couldn't see Dr Haven; the director was sitting behind him on a stool. But he could hear the doctor's calm, steady breathing. That soapy, antiseptic smell was so sharp it prickled his nose.

There was a faint scratching while the director scribbled in his notebook.

"So," said Dr Haven. "Your account matches the one given by Teal and Ruby. Although – somewhat predictably – Teal went into far more detail. He spoke at great length about how the incident will have terrible implications, particularly for his wellbeing and mental health. He'll be absolutely fine, of course, though I had to prescribe a mild sedative."

Cyan lifted his glasses to rub angrily at his eyes, before twisting in the doctor's direction. "Is there any reason our accounts wouldn't match up?"

"Not particularly. I merely need to be thorough in checking what was said and what wasn't. It's just a precaution, to ensure Jonquil didn't say anything that might compromise your respective treatments. But everything looks well and good to me."

"*Well and good?*" Cyan's fringe clung to the sweat on his forehead. "It wasn't well and good at all! It was awful. Did Mr Banter have to be so rough with Jonquil? He could have hurt her!"

Dr Haven's tone was calm, pragmatic. "We did what we had to do, Cyan. Jonquil acted against her treatment, and by doing so she posed a risk not only to herself, but to the rest of you too. We did what was necessary."

Cyan grimaced. Was that why the doctor had lied to him – why he'd tried to wipe the bone message from his memory? Was it somehow *necessary*?

He opened his mouth, close to telling the doctor that he knew what he'd done. But he thought better of it. There might be consequences. And now he'd seen consequences close up.

Cyan thought again about how Mr Banter had handled Jonquil and felt glad about a decision he'd made earlier. He wouldn't tell Dr Haven about the message in cabin 7270. He'd keep it to himself.

Crossing his arms, he returned his gaze to the framed butterflies. "It's not just what Mr Banter did. It's what *I* did too."

His arms began to loosen. Some of the stiffness left his jaw. "I keep replaying it in my head. The way Jonquil screamed. The way she looked at me. She was so scared and…*hurt*. I feel terrible for running away like that – for getting her taken away. It feels like…like I betrayed her."

The doctor's voice was as level as before. "You didn't betray her at all, Cyan. You did the right thing. You helped her by discouraging what she was doing. And in doing so you supported her treatment. In that sense, what you did was the opposite of betraying her."

Cyan shook his head. "It didn't feel like that. It felt like I was…hurting her. As in, properly *hurting* her. She looked at me like I'd just stabbed her in the heart. She was in so much pain." He massaged his jaw with his hands. "She was so desperate to talk. She kept saying how much she… *needed* it."

The doctor scribbled another note. "People usually don't know what they need, Cyan. They don't know what's best for them. That's why the world has doctors. You followed protocol and you helped her. Take pride in that and move on."

A mirthless laugh left Cyan's lips. "I'll never feel proud of it."

"Then at least move on. Spare no further thought for Jonquil. Her initial treatment was too gentle; I suspect that's how this situation arose. It was a blip and it's easily put right. I'll see to it that the sanctuary gives Jonquil… exactly what she needs."

"Where is she now? Is she okay?"

"She's in the medical quarters, recuperating, and she's perfectly fine. She might be out of action for a few days, though, while I administer some additional treatment."

Cyan heard the stool creak. The director went to the cabinets beyond his desk, before returning with a pill and a glass of water. "We're done now, Cyan. Take this before you go. It'll help to calm your nerves."

The pill was in the centre of Cyan's palm. He eyed it for some time and realized he felt wary about putting it in his mouth.

"Is there a problem?" asked the doctor.

Cyan shook his head, swallowed the pill and washed it down. He sat up on the couch, cocking his head. "Doctor?"

"M-hm?"

"Have you noticed there's no…boyfriends or girlfriends here?"

"I have. But what's made you notice?"

"Jonquil asked about it."

"Jonquil brought that up?" A thin huff escaped Dr Haven's nostrils. "I certainly misjudged her initial treatment."

"So what about it?"

"About what?"

*About what…*

Cyan's thoughts were muddled. It was hard to remember what he'd just asked.

He frowned at his knees, trying again. "The…boyfriend and girlfriend thing."

Silence from the director. He tightened his tie a little and smiled softly while explaining. "Certain types of relationship, Cyan, impede the Lethe Method. So we use special means to suppress such –" he trailed off, searching for the word – "urges."

"Oh." Cyan blinked and squinted at Dr Haven. "But doesn't that…" He struggled to gather his thoughts. "Isn't that…sort of…unnatural?" His arms felt limp and light, as if they might float off into the air. "To control people's… feelings like that?"

Cyan blinked slowly at Dr Haven's face, noticing how kindly his smile was. And there was so much detail in his irises. Grey oceans of texture and tone.

The doctor cupped Cyan's elbow to help him to his feet. "You should probably find your room and lie down, Cyan, before your pill kicks in. Would you like me to call Mr Banter so he can help you out?"

Cyan swayed on his feet. He heard someone laugh and say, "Most definitely not," before realizing he'd spoken.

"Rest well, Cyan. You've had a very trying day."

"Sometime…somewhere," breathed Cyan. The door buzzed and he let himself out.

# CAT AND TONGUE

Days went by, blurring and blending in their humdrum way. Uniform colours changed. Rooms, stairways and hallways shifted. Furnishings and fittings came and went. Fittings and furnishings went and came.

Cyan was starting to worry. It felt like a long spell of time – two or three days, perhaps, maybe even a week – had passed, and there'd still been no sign of Jonquil.

So his ears pricked up when, on a day of navy-blue uniforms, he overheard a couple of younger residents, Scarlet and Mustard, talking in the library; apparently Mauve, another resident, had seen Jonquil behind the sanctuary.

Cyan left the library, flew through the foyer and skirted the sanctuary's side. He turned the rear corner and felt a wave of relief the moment he saw her.

She was sitting on one of the benches on the paving that

edged the building, at the cusp where flagstones gave way to sea lavender and sand. Beyond the sand loomed the rock face – grey-green and emerald with moss – that formed the nook of the island's cove.

"Jonquil!" he hollered, but she didn't move.

Cyan plonked himself beside her and gave his broadest grin. "Ahoy there! How's it going? Everything shipshape?" His grin began to slip. "Jonquil?"

It took a while, but gradually she turned her head. Her pupils settled slowly on him.

Gingerly, Cyan patted her hand. "What are you up to? Enjoying the cove?"

The faintest smile edged its way onto Jonquil's lips, and her head revolved, somewhat mechanically, to face the mossy rocks.

"What's up?" asked Cyan. "Cat got your tongue?" He tutted. "What sort of cat does that anyway, running around taking people's tongues? I wonder where it keeps them all. Must be a pretty gross stash." He tried to chuckle, but it came out sounding strained.

Cyan's smile disappeared. He touched Jonquil's hand again. "Hey. I'm sorry about what happened. At the *Serenity*. I… I didn't have any choice. I had no idea they'd be so…so…"

His tongue felt dry and swollen. Too big for his mouth. He raised a hand to his cheek, soothing the heat that flushed there. "It's the rules, you see. We're not supposed to talk about the past. You know that, don't you? It helps us forget."

Jonquil turned her head again to Cyan. That vague smile still lingered on her face. "Forget…" Her voice was like an echo, from somewhere far away. Cyan wasn't sure whether it was the clouds passing overhead, but her eyes seemed to dim.

He nodded encouragingly. "Yeah. Forgetting. That's why you came here. Why we all came here." He touched her hand again. "But still, I'm—"

"Ahoy, you two!" came a lively call from behind.

Cyan turned on the bench to see Ruby approaching. Brushing the curls from her face, she took a seat on the other side of Jonquil. Her leg jiggled beneath her blue skirt. "Nice to see you, Jonquil. It's been…"

She trailed off when Jonquil got up.

Frowning together, Ruby and Cyan watched in silence while Jonquil left them and disappeared around the corner.

Ruby's leg resumed its jiggling. "That was weird."

Cyan's gaze lingered on the corner. "That's nothing. You should have seen her before you turned up. It was like she was…somewhere else. Not quite here."

"Hm." Ruby shrugged. "She's probably just had some strobe therapy. Always spaces you out."

"I guess so. But I've never seen anyone…*that* out of it."

"Must have been a long session."

"Maybe." Cyan tried to sound convinced. "That's probably it."

"Enough about that." Ruby gave his hair a ruffle so fierce it left his glasses askew. "I've got something for you."

She glanced quickly over both shoulders, then slid along the bench to slip something into his blazer pocket.

Cyan moved to reach for whatever it was, but Ruby stopped him.

"What is it?" he asked.

"For later. A little something to help you."

"Help me with what?"

Ruby gestured from his head to his toes. "All this moping! Ever since the *Serenity* thing you've been as much fun as a stubbed toe. And frankly you're boring me." She rolled her eyes and let her tongue hang out.

"I am?"

"You see!" Ruby slapped his arm. "Normally you'd shoot something back at me, but you're all slumpy and dull. Even Teal's more fun than you right now."

The sides of Cyan's mouth drooped. "That bad?"

"Worse. So, that little something in your pocket is there to perk you up." She lowered her voice. "Just promise me you won't touch it 'til tonight, when everyone's asleep."

"Tonight?"

"Just do as I say. You're lucky I'm sharing this with you.

**112**

Earn it, okay? Keep it to yourself."

Cyan gave a shrug. "Fine."

"Goody-good. I'm off, then. Showing Pewter around some caves. Sometime-somewhere!"

Cyan stretched out a hand, but before he could say anything, Ruby had run around the corner and vanished from sight.

# SNUGS AND HOLLOWS

That night, long after residents had followed their lockets to their rooms, Cyan sat upright on his bed. He was still fully dressed in uniform and had a book open in his hands, though he hadn't read a word.

He was staying awake for Ruby, but wouldn't have been able to sleep anyway. Whenever he closed his eyes he saw Jonquil's face, the way it had been by the cove.

Even on previous nights, sleep hadn't come easily. In the quiet darkness, with nothing to distract him, Cyan's thoughts always turned to the same things: codes on bones and notes in drawers; carved messages about past lives and memory thieves.

Cyan lowered his book. He could tell it was late. The Lethe Method may have done away with clocks, but it couldn't stop the silent sluggishness – almost a change in air pressure – that clogs a room when everyone's asleep

**114**

but you. Cyan's current room – like most of the sanctuary's bedrooms – had no window. But he could *feel* that all was still on the dunes.

Leaving his book face-down on the pillow, Cyan reached warily into his blazer and pulled out a folded sheet of paper, with what he assumed was Ruby's writing on its front:

*Are you SURE everyone's asleep?*

Cyan shoved the note beneath his armpit and checked the door was still shut. Residents weren't allowed pens or paper. He had no idea how Ruby had got hold of both.

After listening out carefully, he withdrew the sheet and unfolded it to find a list of instructions.

*1. Are you REALLY sure everyone's asleep?*

Cyan rolled his eyes.

*2. Go into one of your room's snugs but make sure you LEAVE YOUR LOCKET in its charger.*

Cyan contemplated his locket, which was slotted into the charger on the bed's headboard. He rubbed his lips doubtfully, shrugged to himself, then entered the snug in a vertical section of the room's frame. He felt uneasy without his locket, but distracted himself by reading the next instruction.

*3. Feel around the lip at the bottom of the snug. You'll find two small hollows. Press them at the same time.*

Cyan crouched and did as the sheet instructed. It took

some fumbling, but to his surprise he found two subtle dents, tucked out of sight within the ebony grooves. He pushed them both and heard a quiet click from somewhere within the frame.

His chin dropped when a section of the snug's rear slid backwards and sideways, to reveal a hole large enough to climb through.

After staring at the opening for at least a minute, Cyan slowly lifted Ruby's sheet to his face.

*4. In you go.*

He snorted a laugh and backed slowly out from the snug. His eyes skimmed the next instruction.

*5. If you're backing away you're a phony. All those times you've made fun of Teal for being chicken! So go on. Get in. I DARE you.*

"Dares me?" Cyan snorted another laugh. "She honestly thinks I'm going to fall for that?"

He looked back and forth between the opening and the bed, then cursed beneath his breath and re-entered the snug. He looked again at the instructions while there was light from his room.

*6. You in? Good. Knew you would. Climb onto the ladder in the shaft behind the snug. Remember the code next to the opening you've come through (DON'T forget it!) and climb up. Keep going until you reach the top. I'll hear you when you get there.*

Cyan clicked his tongue and – after slipping the

instructions back into his pocket – got to his knees to poke his head through the opening. He peered down into a metal shaft with ladders attached to each of its four sides. It was hard to tell how deep the shaft went; the lights trailing the ladders were small and dim.

Tightening his lips, Cyan climbed through the opening and onto the nearest ladder. After making a mental note of the code stencilled next to the opening – *GC5* – he began to move upwards.

As his eyes adjusted, he noticed horizontal shafts that regularly met his own, extending away in four opposite directions. He also clocked the steel cables stretched tautly along pulleys in every shaft. It was only after climbing a while longer that it really hit him: he was climbing *within* the framework that both supported and shuffled the upper rooms.

Cyan's heart stopped and he reached uselessly for his pocket, fumbling for the locket he'd left behind, before reminding himself that the floors never shuffled overnight. Even so, he shuddered and picked up his pace.

He sensed a change in the light not far above – a darkness more blue than black – and was soon climbing from the ladder's top onto a metal gangway. Even though he was still indoors, Cyan felt a metallic chill in the air. Buttoning his blazer, he crept carefully along and peered about the gloom.

He was on one of countless criss-crossing gangways, which all led to other shafts with their own sets of ladders. Immense metal cogs, gears and pulleys filled the rails above Cyan's head, fanning out into indigo distance.

"About time."

The voice startled him and he grabbed a rail to stop himself from falling.

"Made you jump." A dark outline appeared by some cogs.

"Ruby!"

She raised her finger to her lips and Cyan slapped a hand over his mouth. His voice dropped to a hiss while he pointed at the shaft by his feet. "You nearly killed me!"

"Better luck next time."

"Not funny."

"Welcome, by the way. What do you think?" Ruby opened her arms and twirled on the spot.

Cyan peered again into the gloom. "It's… It… We're at the top of the framework, aren't we?"

A slow clap from Ruby. "You're smarter than you look. Doesn't take much, though."

"How'd you find out how to get in here?"

"Happened a while back. I dropped my locket in a snug during a shuffle. My finger brushed one of the hollows, so I started exploring. I found the second hollow and…*voilà*. Hey, do you know the number of the opening you climbed through?"

"GC5."

"Good. Shaft GC'll take you back to your room. You left your locket there, right?"

"Yeah. Why'd I have to leave it?"

"So no one knows we left our rooms."

"How do you mean?" Cyan's eyebrows drew together. "Hang on. Are you saying…"

"Yeah, the staff can track our lockets."

Cyan's head pulled back. "You really think so?"

"Well, *duh.*" Ruby rapped his forehead with her knuckles. "You're such an idiot. If your locket can tell you where things are, it must be telling something else where *it* is. It's called logic, Cyan. Try it some time. And you saw how the helicopter came when you called for help, didn't you? The staff knew *exactly* where you were."

Cyan frowned at the memory of that day. "Oh. Right."

Ruby turned away and started walking. "Come on. Got something to show you."

DOSE FOURTEEN

# DUNE-LIGHT

Ruby spoke in hushed tones while Cyan trailed her along
gangways. "Just so you know: if you go down the ladders
instead of up –" she pointed at a nearby shaft – "they'll take
you to the engine floor, where they have all the mechanisms
for moving the rooms. Cogs and machines and stuff. It's
pretty awesome. There're even stairs which I *think* go from
there to the communal and staff floors. But I don't go to
the engine floor much. Once there was a technician
hanging around with a clipboard. Getting caught sneaking
around the framework probably wouldn't go down well.
God knows what Ms Ferryman would say."

"Or Dr Haven." That word came again to Cyan's mind:
*consequences*.

He unbuttoned his blazer, suddenly warm in the cool
air. "Don't you think it's risky to be here?"

"Probably."

Cyan patted his blazer pocket. "And what about your note? Where'd you even *get* a pen and paper?"

"They're Ms Ferryman's. I had a meeting in her office. Sort of…borrowed them while her back was turned."

Cyan huffed. "Great. So we'll get in trouble for being here *and* for using notes."

"Chill out, Teal."

"I'm *not* Teal."

"No, Teal's more fun."

Cyan was about to respond but had nothing to come back with. He pushed his hands into his pockets. "It just seems risky, that's all."

"It's worth it. Take a look through that window."

She'd led Cyan to the far end of the space, where large round windows were embedded regularly along the concrete wall. Cyan put his palms on the nearest window's deep, circular cavity and leaned forward to put his face to the glass.

The sanctuary's top was so high up that he could see sand dunes unfolding beneath him. They stretched out into the distance, with the moon perched above the curving horizon. Beneath the moon's belly a white beam coursed across sand, just as it would a moonlit sea.

Ruby spoke from behind. "You like it?"

Cyan barely heard her. The moon quilted the dunes with spectral salt-sparkle. He saw tiny whale skeletons and ship shadows, twinkling like the stars above the sands. And a distant column of darkness – the *Serenity*…

Ruby smacked her lips. "Wow. I've actually found something that shuts you up."

Cyan turned his head to look at her. "Man alive, Ruby. It's…beautiful."

"I know. And I'm not keen on sharing it either. But I made an exception for you. Thought it might stop you being such a wet blanket."

She shoved Cyan aside and – after climbing into the cavity to rest against its curve – sat with her arms around her legs. Cyan mirrored her pose on the cavity's other side and they stared in silence through the glass.

Moments passed by, until Ruby kicked Cyan's shin.

"Ow!"

"So what is it, misery guts?" Ruby's legs jittered behind her folded arms. "You're not seriously still moping over what happened at the *Serenity*, are you?"

Cyan wished that was all that was troubling him. He fidgeted against the concrete, tempted to tell all. The bone code and drawer. What the doctor had done…

But he bit his tongue. If what he knew carried any threat of consequences, could he really pass that risk on to Ruby?

He lowered his eyes.

Ruby sucked air in through her teeth. "Stop stressing about it, okay? You did the right thing for Jonquil. Letting her talk could have ruined her treatment. And she's out and about again now. All's well that ends well, right?"

Cyan turned his face to the window. "But *has* it ended well? You saw her earlier. Don't you think something was really…off about her?"

"Like I said, we probably caught her after some treatment."

Cyan pursed his lips. "Maybe. But…" He fell silent.

When he spoke again, his voice was so low Ruby had to lean in to hear. "Do you ever wonder…" He hesitated again.

"Hm?"

"Do you ever wonder about what we're doing here? I mean…about the forgetting?"

"Why would I?"

Cyan met her gaze. "Some…stuff's got me thinking about it. Not just Jonquil. Other stuff too."

Ruby looked puzzled. "What stuff?"

Cyan lifted his glasses, trying to rub the tiredness from his eyes.

"I'm finding it harder and harder," he finally said, "to ignore the fact I'm feeling…bothered."

Ruby cocked her head. "In what way?"

"That's part of the problem. I know some of the stuff that bothers me…" Again he resisted the urge to tell her what Dr Haven had done, and thought instead about the whale bones and cabin.

"When I get certain…feelings," he went on, remembering how his hands had trembled when he'd read the note in the drawer, "I can't figure out why I'm feeling them. It's like there's a no-zone in my head. I find it really hard to focus on stuff like that. Do you know what I mean?" Cyan looked imploringly into Ruby's face. "Does that make any sense at all?"

Ruby still looked puzzled, but Cyan caught her expression faltering. She was trying to hide something.

He leaned forward to look more closely at her face. "You *do* know what I mean."

Ruby pulled back. She took a deep breath, then let it out slowly through her nose. "Not really. I'm not worried or anything. I do have this…thing, though. But I'm not supposed to talk about it."

Cyan's eyebrows rose. "Why not?"

Ruby looked away. "In case it…" She stopped, shook her head and crossed her arms. "No, I can't—"

"*In case*," interrupted Cyan, quoting what the doctor said so often about his fear of fire, "other people interfere and hinder your progress."

Ruby's arms unfolded. Her eyes were large and on Cyan again. "How do you know that?"

"Because I've got a thing too, and I'm told exactly the same. By Dr Haven, right?" He watched her closely. "So what's the thing you're told to keep to yourself?"

Ruby's lips were clenched.

Cyan put his hand out, touched the toe of her plimsoll. "It's all right. I'll make it fair. Will you tell me yours if I tell you mine?"

Again, Ruby's expression weakened.

"Okay," said Cyan. "I suffer from pyrophobia."

"Pyro-what?"

"A fear of fire."

"Oh," breathed Ruby. Something softened in her eyes. She looked through the window, towards the distant pillar of darkness. "So that's why you never light the fire. By the *Serenity*."

"Yep. And just like with you, Dr Haven tells me to keep it secret."

Ruby looked sad. Cyan touched her toe again. "Want to tell me yours?"

Ruby stared at him and gnawed her lower lip. Again, she took a long, deep breath. She flicked some curls from her face and her gaze fell. "I… I get down sometimes."

"Down? Like sad?"

"More than sad. Like *really* down. Sometimes I feel sort of…abandoned, I guess. Which I know sounds stupid."

"It doesn't sound stupid at all."

Ruby smiled faintly, then carried on. "I get this wave of emptiness. A big, sad emptiness that makes me go to my room and lie on the bed. And when I get there, I feel pinned down. Like a bug or something. I can't get up. Not for a long time. And what makes it worse is there's not even any real abandonment. It makes no sense."

Cyan rocked forward and back again. "Just like my pyrophobia."

"Yeah. It's like you said. I know *what* I feel, but I can't figure out why. And then…" She trailed off, grimacing at Cyan before looking at her knees. "I've told you too much."

"It's okay. Stop if you want. And thanks. I know it's not easy."

Ruby nodded slowly to herself, then looked up again. "We'd better shut up before we start…you know, *interfering* even more with each other's treatment."

When Cyan smiled he meant it. "I actually feel better after all this interfering."

Ruby smiled back. "Yeah. I guess I do as well." She shrugged. "But what do we know?"

Cyan couldn't answer. Frowning, he tipped his head back against the coolness of the curve. "Don't you think it's weird, though, that both of us have these things Dr Haven tells us to keep secret? Doesn't it make you wonder whether other residents are hiding problems? Whether they're told to pretend they're fine too?"

Ruby gave a quiet laugh. "What? Like Teal? Yeah, he's always pretending he's fine."

"But Teal only goes on about surface stuff – the little

things. Maybe his worrying's worse than we realize. Did you see the state of him when everything kicked off with Jonquil? He was properly, like, *shaking*. Maybe all his stressing comes from…from something deeper."

Cyan turned his face away, then realized he'd done so in shame, thinking of all the times he'd teased Teal. He could just make out his reflection in the glass, and he gazed at it glumly. "I mean, if the way Teal gets is even a *tiny* bit like the way I've been feeling…"

He sighed and straightened, with his eyes once more on Ruby. "What I'm saying is, for all we know, *loads* of residents could be hiding problems. It'd be a weird coincidence if it's just us two and we ended up talking about it tonight."

"Coincidences do happen, Cyan."

"I'm not so sure. Sometimes it makes me wonder. You know, about the trust we put in Dr Haven. Whether there's something…going on. Something sort of…"

He trailed off when he saw Ruby gaping at him, as if struck by a horrific realization. Her mouth began to open, and she cupped a hand around her chin while leaning close. Her voice dropped to a shaky whisper. "Oh my god. I'll tell you what's *really* weird…"

Cyan stared back and tilted his ear to her lips. He could feel the muscles tightening around his neck and shoulders. "What?" he hissed. "What's weird?"

"*You*, you freak!" Ruby hooted and leaned back against

the cavity, chuckling and snorting while Cyan pouted.

"God, Cyan! This is even worse than I imagined. I thought you were just getting *boring*. Turns out you're paranoid too! Talk about overthinking things. You really *are* worse than Teal!"

Cyan was still pouting. But as he watched Ruby grin and roll her eyes, he couldn't fight the smile that crept onto his lips.

He shrugged and allowed his shoulders to loosen. Ruby was still chortling and Cyan wondered whether she might be right. Perhaps he *had* been overthinking things. Overreacting. Making mountains of molehills. There was no harm in hoping.

Groaning tiredly, he kicked Ruby's toe with his own. "Thanks, by the way. For showing me this." He nodded at the window.

Ruby kicked his toe in return and cocked an eyebrow. "Stop obsessing and try to relax, yeah? It'll be good to have the old Cyan back one day – as annoying as he was."

Grinning, she turned her attention to the window. Cyan saw the silvery light on her face. He smiled too and joined her in gazing at the sandscape.

"Just look at it," sighed Ruby. "It's like a frozen sea – the way the dunes make waves in the moonlight."

"Dune-light," said Cyan, almost to himself.

Ruby beamed. "Yeah. Dune-light. That's perfect."

# MUSTARD AND STARCH

The next evening, after being called to the canteen by his locket, Cyan joined Ruby and Teal in the queue for food. They'd landed the same dinner shift.

The canteen that day was lit by paper lanterns, which hung in sprawling clusters from the ceiling. Some mahogany booths had been set up along the walls; the trio jumped into one before it could be seized by anyone else.

Cyan and Teal shared a long seat, with their mustard-yellow uniforms bright against the booth's green padding. Ruby sat on the opposite side and joined the boys in downing a dose of pills.

Cyan was chewing chicken when someone caught his eye. "Jonquil!" he called. "You want to sit with us?" He leaned out and waved, but Jonquil passed the booth and kept walking.

Cyan sensed Ruby watching him. He glanced across to catch her looking concerned, though she quickly wrinkled her nose. "You shouldn't talk with your mouth full," she said. "It's gross."

Cyan pulled a face. "You gabble with your mouth full all the time. It's like talking to a food blender."

Ruby hooted. "Food in my mouth makes conversation with you bearable. At least that way there's *something* interesting going on."

Cyan scoffed. "That's actually not a bad idea." He scooped a huge lump of food into his mouth and could barely speak through his risotto. "You're right! You're… almost bearable…like this."

Ruby had already refilled her mouth. "Good! I'm glad we've – " she almost gagged while trying to speak – "found a…way to be…bearable."

They were both already chortling, and laughed all the harder when food fell from their mouths back onto their plates.

Teal didn't look impressed. He picked up his tray and edged away. "You two are disgusting. You're getting germs everywhere."

Ruby grinned. "A few germs are good for you. In fact…" She plucked a clump of rice from her mouth, and was offering it to Teal when a strangled cry made all three of them turn their heads.

Cyan's heart missed a beat. He knew that cry from the *Serenity*. It was Jonquil.

Other residents were swivelling on their seats. There was some sort of commotion at the food counter. Throwing his cutlery down, Cyan slid from the booth and jumped onto a chair. He saw Jonquil swinging a metal tray at some residents, who were staggering backwards with their hands shielding their faces.

Jonquil howled like an injured animal. Mangled words broke up her cries, but they were hard to hear over the crowd's startled chatter. Through the pounding of blood in his ears, Cyan heard her shout something about a sister, about forgetting – about losing too much.

With her eyes rolling and spit on her chin, Jonquil clutched a handful of forks and hurled them at a nearby table. She clamped her lips together, but struggled to keep her mouth shut, as if in battle with her own voice.

Cyan was already squeezing past stunned residents. As he drew nearer, he found himself frozen by the terror in Jonquil's eyes. She hugged the tray against her chest. A violent shaking took command of her limbs.

Three orderlies in starched white uniforms pushed through the crowd. They surrounded Jonquil, only to fall back when she swiped with her tray and sent one of them toppling.

Jonquil trembled, stuttered and swayed. The noise from the crowd grew louder. Cyan's head swept desperately left and right, and he saw Dr Haven speaking calmly into his staff locket. A moment later there was movement by the canteen entrance. Residents were making way for Mr Banter, who strode through the crowd in his usual leisurely way.

Jonquil shrank from the blond orderly's steady, looming approach, but the food counter left her with nowhere to go. Mr Banter took her arm in his hand and she lashed out with her tray. There was a resounding clang as it crashed against his head.

The orderly's thick glasses were cracked and bent, though other than that, nothing in his cool, faintly amused expression changed. With his free hand, he pinched the tray's edge between finger and thumb, plucked it away and tossed it aside.

Jonquil was shaking all over. She could barely keep her eyes on the cartridge Mr Banter pulled from his pocket. When a long needle sprang from its top, a confused gasp rippled through the crowd. Cyan felt a sickly rush of heat and pushed again towards Jonquil.

He whimpered, almost in pain, when Mr Banter jammed the needle into Jonquil's neck. Her body seemed to cramp and contract, before becoming limp and crumpling in the orderly's arms.

Cyan tried to follow while Mr Banter dragged Jonquil to the exit, but his way was blocked by shocked residents. Orderlies were filtering through the crowd and calmly offering pills.

Some residents – mostly younger ones – obediently swallowed their pills and sank to the floor. Others were resisting, waving their arms, raising their voices. Cyan saw them silenced by needles, before they stiffened and collapsed like stringless puppets.

He glanced back towards his booth, saw Teal and Ruby slumped with their faces in their food. Looking ahead again, he spotted the top of Mr Banter's head and leaped over a sprawled resident before rebounding from an orderly's chest.

"Take this, Cyan." The orderly held out an oval blue pill. His mouth was twisted into a smile, but the eyes beneath his fringe were dark and determined.

"Jonquil…" pleaded Cyan. He threw a finger towards her. "What happened? Is she… Will she be okay?"

"Just take this, Cyan. Then everything will be fine."

Cyan pushed himself on tiptoes to peer over the orderly's shoulder. "I can't. It's Jonquil. I just want to… I need to know…"

The orderly grumbled through gritted teeth. There was a cold sting in Cyan's neck, and his muscles tightened around his bones, as if snaring him in a net.

And then: numbness and nothing.

# PINS

*Beep.*

   *Beep.*

      *Beep.*

         *Beep.*

On it went. A muted chorus of beeps and bleeps.

Cyan awoke to whiteness – to a sparse white ceiling, white halogen strip lights, the cruel glare of white-tiled walls.

He moved his hand to his stomach, trying to ease the nausea there, and in doing so realized his limbs were sore, and that he was wearing a grey hospital gown.

With a groan, he sat up slowly and put a hand to his aching head. The chill air made him cross his arms and hug himself. He noticed his tortoiseshell glasses by his pillow, put them on and looked around to see a wall-mounted sink, a table and a handful of trolleys, all stainless steel and bright in sterile light. A large metal cabinet sat some way to his left, and on his right…

Cyan shivered at the sight of Teal and Ruby, unconscious on metal trolley beds, connected by wires to various consoles. He shifted on his own trolley bed to look closer. They were breathing slowly but steadily. Metallic pads were attached to their temples. Thin wires left the necks of their gowns, and they each wore a plastic clip on one of their fingers. Further wires dangled from the clips, joining the cables that snaked their way to beeping monitors.

Cyan reached up, felt metal pads on his own temples and instinctively yanked them off. He did the same with the pad taped to his chest and the clip on his finger, and was startled by a loud buzzing from one of the monitors.

One of the room's two doors opened and Dr Haven appeared. His polished shoes clopped briskly across the linoleum floor, and he silenced the buzzing with a tap of a console. He studied the various monitors while speaking. "Excellent. You're awake."

Cyan squinted at the back of the doctor's black, long-tailed coat. Fuzzy memories were returning. Residents and orderlies. The crash and clatter of cutlery.

"The canteen," mumbled Cyan. "What…happened?"

Dr Haven turned and smiled contentedly. "Nothing of concern. A minor inconvenience. How are you feeling?"

Cyan smacked his parched lips. "Thirsty. Can I have a drink?"

"All in good time." The doctor dragged a metal chair across the floor and sat himself in front of Cyan. "I hope you don't mind me allowing you to wake up before your treatment begins."

"Treatment?"

"I need to ask you some questions. While you're still able to answer them." Dr Haven crossed one leg over the other, opened his notebook and took a pen from his coat. "Did you talk to Jonquil much? After the incident at the *Serenity*, I mean."

"Um." Cyan's forehead wrinkled while he tried to recollect. "I tried, I guess. By the back of the cove. But it was hard to get much out of her."

"M-hm. And what exactly *did* you get out of her?"

Cyan opened his mouth to reply, but his breath caught in his throat. He was hit by an image of Jonquil, screaming and trembling by the food counter. And Mr Banter, with a flashing needle…

He felt his heart throbbing harder. Much of his grogginess evaporated and he became intensely aware of the room's thin, sterilized air. Bile churned painfully in the pit of his stomach.

The doctor encouraged him with a waft of his pen. Cyan winced and pushed a palm against his forehead. "Hang on.

Where *is* Jonquil?"

Dr Haven spoke with his eyes on his pad. "She's around."

Cyan glanced about. "But where?"

"Near enough. No more than a few...rooms away." The director put the pen briefly to his lips. "Now tell me, Cyan: what did Jonquil say to you, when she saw fit to speak? Did she try to talk again about her past?"

Cyan wiped damp hair from his forehead. He looked again at Ruby and Teal, unconscious and wired up on their beds. "Where...are we? Have we left the sanctuary?"

"No."

"Really?" Cyan straightened his glasses, searching the room for familiar signs. "I've never seen this place before."

"You have, but you don't remember."

"What?"

The doctor drummed the top of his pen against his pad. "Let's focus on the matter at hand, Cyan. Now tell me: did Jonquil try again to talk about her history? Did she ever say anything about how she was feeling, physically or mentally?"

"What's happening here? Why are Ruby and Teal unconscious?"

"That's not what we're discussing now."

"I have a right to know, though, don't I?"

Dr Haven tapped his notepad again with his pen, but

this time harder. His smile stiffened, just a little. "Actually, you don't. There are certain rights you signed away when you began your treatment. Not that you'll remember. But take my word for it: rights can be more damaging to people than they know. So, forget about why we're here and answer my questions."

Cyan straightened up. His cheeks and palms were getting hot. "Let me see Jonquil first. I want to know she's okay."

Dr Haven tutted lightly and released a curt breath through his nostrils. "You can't see Jonquil. It'll be for the best when everyone's forgotten about her."

"Forgotten about her?" Cyan stared at the doctor. "Is... Wait a minute. Is that what you meant? When you said you wanted to ask me questions...while I'm still able to answer?" His gaze returned to Ruby and Teal. "Are you wiping our memories of Jonquil?"

The director blinked slowly, got up from his chair and strolled to the stainless-steel sink. "I've already removed the other residents' memories of the period since Jonquil arrived. The last thing we want is for them to feel unsettled by what happened." The basin pinged while he gave his hands a thorough wash. "I postponed the treatment of you, Teal and Ruby, so that I could gather some information for my notes on Jonquil; you three seemed closest to her. But you're proving to be just like the other two before I put them under sedation again: not useful at all. So let's move things along, shall we?"

"But…" Cyan couldn't find words. He watched while Dr Haven dried his hands on a paper towel, crossed the room and opened the steel cabinet.

When the cabinet door closed, the doctor was holding a large glass syringe.

Cyan saw transparent fluid in the syringe's barrel, before his eyes were drawn to its thick, glistening needle. He swivelled from his bed, put bare feet on the cold floor. "Is that what's going to wipe my memory? Of Jonquil?"

"It is." That calm, contented smile had settled again on Dr Haven's face. "Our little talk today will be removed too, of course."

"But what about…" Cyan was edging along his trolley bed. "What'll happen to Jonquil? Will she be okay?"

The doctor sighed, though not without amusement. "Most probably not."

# NEEDLES

Cyan froze. A wave of dizziness made him grip the metal bedframe. "What? But..." He swallowed sorely. "What's wrong with her? Is she ill?"

"She's certainly not well."

"In what way?"

The director shrugged gently, took a step forward with his syringe.

Cyan edged further along the bed. "*Please.* Tell me."

Dr Haven regarded Cyan. His smile was as sly as it was subtle. "I'll keep it simple for you," he said. "While the Lethe Method can very adeptly remove people's memories, there's often a stubborn...residue that lingers. Emotional dregs, if you will. And they're much more difficult to remove than the memories that created them. Hence, for example, your special relationship with fire."

"Wha—" Cyan's mouth flapped open and shut,

but nothing else came.

"Fear of fire is just the tip of your iceberg, Cyan. There are emotions you have that you're not even aware of. Emotions the Lethe Method tucks deeply away."

Warm sweat was beading on Cyan's forehead. "Tucks away?" He pushed a hand against his chest, trying to slow his racing heart. "But…the fire… It's a phobia. It's nothing to do with my past. You… You said so!"

"I say whatever's necessary. And your phobia has everything to do with your past. I know you better than you know yourself, Cyan. I have your resident's file. I know all about your history, about your parents."

Cyan's breaths came out in gasps. "My parents?" Hot pain flared suddenly behind his eyes. He blinked it away, shook his head aggressively. "But these…emotional dregs… What have they got to do with Jonquil?"

"As I mentioned, most of them we can keep deeply hidden. But their repression can have…" The doctor hesitated. "Actually, I think I've told you enough."

"*Tell me.*" Cyan's fists began clenching by his sides. He could feel his anger rising. Fury bubbled beneath his fear. "Or are you scared of saying something you shouldn't?" He nodded at the syringe. "Is there a chance I'll remember?"

Dr Haven raised his chin, just a little, then blinked several times, in quick succession. He smiled at the liquid in the syringe. "Oh, there's no chance you'll remember."

Cyan sensed a chink in the doctor's armour. "Then why not tell me what happened to Jonquil?"

"I have a lot to attend to, Cyan. Speaking further would be a waste of time."

Cyan nodded again at the needle. "Because of what you'll do with that?" He rolled back his shoulders and forced all the conviction he could into his voice. "I don't think it's as reliable as you say. I think you don't want to say more because your methods aren't good enough."

Cyan had no doubt the drug in the syringe would work. But he went on goading as best as he could, pushing at the only vulnerability open to him: the director's arrogance. "They've failed you before," he went on. "I know what you did. You tried to remove my memory. Of what I found on the whale bones. But it didn't work."

The doctor's thin lips parted, but for once he seemed lost for words. His eyebrows sank darkly. "I beg your pardon?"

"So much for your ethical code. And so much for your stupid strobes. *That's* why you won't tell me. You're scared to. Your gimmicks and gadgets aren't reliable."

The light was harsh enough to expose a faint reddening in Dr Haven's cheeks. He considered Cyan with eyes like grey marbles, then spoke firmly through stiffening lips. "I'm not entirely sure how you remember the message on those bones, Cyan. I can only assume some rogue trigger restored the memory; strobe therapy works over gradual sessions, and I was working with limited data." He pointed his syringe at Cyan. "But that's not the case today. This drug is thorough, quick and *completely* reliable. So I'll finish what I was saying, Cyan, and I'll do so because you *will* forget."

The director took a deep breath. His cheeks dulled from pink to grey. "The repression of certain emotions – not just those left by the forgotten trauma, but also anxieties that sometimes develop here on the island – can lead to complications. It creates hidden tensions: emotional conflict and confusion, of which the patient mostly isn't aware. And this pressure can express itself in various ways, some of which are mild – the whitening of your hair, for example, or Teal's obsessive fretting – and some of which become more extreme, as we saw in Jonquil. She's an unfortunate casualty of the method. Damaged goods."

Cyan's eyes were agape. "So the treatment can be... *harmful?*"

"For now – until I determine how to iron out its flaws."

"*Its flaws?* But what about Jonquil? What if more residents get hurt? You can't do that!"

"Actually I can. That's essentially what you all signed up for."

"You give us pills before we sign! I saw you do it with Jonquil. What do those pills do?"

"I don't have to tell you. That's another right you signed away."

Cyan threw his hands into his hair. "So the sanctuary… It's just a big…*experiment* for you?" He gestured at Ruby and Teal. "And all the residents – we're just your lab rats?"

"It's an experiment for now. But when the treatment is perfected it will be an immensely profitable business. Can you imagine how much people will pay to have their worst memories removed? For the gift of genuinely selective memory? That's why our investors pour millions into this little…enterprise."

Cyan was speechless again. The syringe's needle glinted when the director took another step towards him. "Enough chit-chat, Cyan. It's time to take your medicine."

Cyan stepped back, with wide eyes fixed on the syringe. "No!" He looked about the room, glanced at Teal and Ruby on their trolley beds. "I can't forget all this!"

The director's expression was kind. Almost benevolent. "I assure you, you can. And won't it be nice? Instantaneous peace of mind. What you don't know can't hurt you." He put a finger to his lower lip. "Actually, it can. But you know what I mean."

He gave the syringe a little shake. "I have something here to knock you senseless and make you forget any of this ever happened. You can go back to climbing shipwrecks and playing in the sand. Now give me your arm."

Cyan glared while Dr Haven gripped his wrist. But as soon as the needle came close he swiped with his free hand, so that the syringe flew from the doctor's fingers.

Together, they watched it roll with a brittle chime across the floor.

A rising grey eyebrow. "So. You'd prefer to do this the hard way. Very well. Mr Banter *likes* the hard way." Dr Haven's hand went to his coat pocket, but the moment he removed his staff locket, Cyan slapped it to the floor as well.

The doctor narrowed his eyes at Cyan. He moved to recover the locket, but faltered when Cyan grabbed a metal chair and aimed its legs at him.

Director and resident glared silently at one another, until Cyan pivoted the chair suddenly in his hands. He slammed the chair's foot again and again against the locket's silver casing. A fierce clanging ricocheted across tiles.

Dr Haven looked first at the locket's remains on the floor, and then at the legs of the chair, which were aimed at him once more. Cyan's breaths came quick and sharp.

The doctor tilted his head, before smoothing some of the hair that bordered his bald patch. He adjusted his tie, turned on his heels and headed for the door from which he'd come.

"Where are you going?" called Cyan.

"To fetch Mr Banter. I don't need a locket to bring him here. There's more than one way to skin a cat. And even more ways to skin a lab rat."

In no rush at all, Dr Haven left the room. Cyan caught a glimpse of the corridor outside – of concrete walls and a stained linoleum floor – before the door slammed shut.

Cyan stood frozen for several moments, his chair still poised in the air. His chest rose and fell beneath his gown, until he threw the chair aside and ran to try the door handle. It was locked. He spun around, searching the room, then ran to the door on its opposite side. That was locked too.

Cyan's sweat felt hot on his skin. His pupils darted about the room, before settling on the syringe he'd knocked from Dr Haven's hand.

Panting rapidly, he ran to the syringe and crouched to pick it up. He eyed the transparent liquid in its barrel, looking closely at the size of the dose, then dashed to the metal sink. With hands shaking, he squirted the syringe's contents into the plug hole. He turned on the tap and – after drawing water up through the syringe's needle – squirted a little back out again, so that the quantity looked the same.

He skidded across the room and put the syringe on the floor, in the same position it had been before.

It didn't take long for Dr Haven to return with Mr

Banter. Cyan was ready for them, with his chair hoisted again.

Dr Haven gestured at the syringe. "If you'd be so kind, Mr Banter."

Mr Banter smiled blandly while strolling to the syringe and picking it up. As he closed in, Cyan grimaced at the needle extending from the glass barrel. His words trembled when he spoke. "Does the needle really need to be so big?"

Mr Banter paused and looked back towards Dr Haven. The doctor's smile curled upwards. "Actually, no. It doesn't."

Cyan swung the chair with all his strength, but it was blocked by Mr Banter's palm, then plucked away like a toy. It clattered across the room, and Cyan was swallowed by the orderly's approach.

His pupils darted to Dr Haven. "Just tell me first! Before I forget! What'll happen to Jonquil?"

"Oh, she'll remain at the sanctuary – though out of sight and out of mind. She still has her uses. Just because a lab rat is damaged, it doesn't mean you can't take it apart for study. We learn as much from our failures as from our successes, don't you think?"

Cyan felt sudden, crushing pain and glanced down. His wrist had disappeared in Mr Banter's fist, which looked grotesquely pink in the room's white light. Cyan cried out at the needle's cold sting, saw the plunger drop, closed his eyes and slumped to the floor.

His arm throbbed with hot, prickling pain. It took all of Cyan's willpower to feign unconsciousness. He heard Dr Haven speaking. "Put him back on the trolley while I prepare something. He could do with an extra sedative to keep him out of trouble; I've had more than my fill of that brat today. Oh, and fetch his file from next door, will you? I'd like to add some notes."

Large hands fumbled beneath Cyan's chest and waist. The ground fell away, before the rubbery softness of a mattress came up to meet him.

There were footsteps, another sting in the arm, and everything went away.

TREATMENT PHASE C

# AWAKENING

*Beep.*

*Beep.*

*Beep.*

*Beep.*

Cyan became aware of muffled sounds. Something wet was clinging to his forehead.

He stirred where he lay, forcing his heavy eyelids open, just a crack. Daylight hit his pupils and he gasped in pain.

He pulled himself up and blinked, willing his eyes to adjust to the light. Murmured sounds floated through the air, and when the glare died away he found himself in blurred but familiar surroundings. Deep-set circular windows. Beds with wheels and raised wooden guards. Cabinets and drawers, vases of sea lavender…

He was in the sanctuary's medical quarters. The last

time he'd been here he'd broken his ankle, after falling from a ledge in one of the island's caves.

"…to cool you down."

A voice by his ear. He jerked away, with hands shooting up to guard his face, then saw Ms Ferryman, the sanctuary's head orderly, sitting by his side.

Her forehead was creased with concern. She put aside the flannel she'd been holding to his head and handed him his tortoiseshell glasses.

Cyan snatched the glasses and slipped them on. He noticed the needle buried deep in his hand, which was connected by tubing to a suspended bag of liquid.

Blinking behind his glasses, Cyan looked around once more. He was sitting up on a bed, with white sheets rumpled around his legs, and still wore a grey hospital gown. The other beds were empty. He and Ms Ferryman were alone.

"Easy," hushed Ms Ferryman. "Try not to strain yourself. I'll call for Dr Haven."

Cyan's fingers gripped the mattress. "Dr Haven…" He tried groggily to swivel from the bed, but Ms Ferryman stopped him with a hand on his knee.

"Stay put and relax. It's normal to feel confused. You're coming out of a nasty fever."

"Fever?"

"You've been out cold for a few days. But you're fine. The director's been keeping a close eye on you."

Cyan shook his head, his breaths quickening. "Dr Haven. He—" He stopped himself, suddenly remembering how much – or how little – he was supposed to know.

Ms Ferryman smiled and tipped her head, so that a black braid slipped from the bun in her hair. "Hm?"

Cyan swallowed drily, adjusted his glasses. "Is there food? I could eat a horse." He attempted a smile, though it made his head throb. "Anything that's not horse would do, though."

Ms Ferryman patted his knee. "It's a good sign that you have an appetite." She stood up, took her locket from her tunic and opened it to speak. "Dr Haven?" She waited a moment. "He's awake."

She restored the locket to her tunic while addressing Cyan. "I'll have the canteen throw something together for you. Perhaps some soup, so you can ease yourself back into eating. Sound good?"

Cyan nodded.

Ms Ferryman headed for the door. As she left the room she spoke to someone in the corridor, though Cyan couldn't make out the words.

The door opened again, and Dr Haven entered.

Cyan's muscles cramped around his neck. A stinging warmth blossomed across his palms and face and – realizing he'd have to hide his fear – he seized the flannel and spread it across his chin and reddening cheeks.

He forced himself to breathe at a more natural pace, shifting against his pillow as Dr Haven closed the door.

The director crossed the room and stopped by Cyan's bed. He looked down from above, beaming gently.

Cyan looked up and feigned a smile. "Ahoy, Doctor." He tapped vaguely at the tip of his non-existent cap, then wished he'd saluted less timidly.

"Hello, Cyan. You're awake."

"Yep. Unless this is a really boring dream."

"Very droll." The director cracked his knuckles and eyed Cyan's flannel. "Are you feeling too warm?"

"A bit. Must be what's left of the fever."

"Ms Ferryman told you."

"Yes."

"And how are you faring?"

"Achy. But not too bad."

Dr Haven studied him with grey, glacial eyes. "Is that all?"

Cyan's forehead furrowed. "I guess so. Shouldn't it be?"

"Your influenza was quite severe."

Cyan shrugged. "If you're going to do something, you might as well do it properly."

"And what do you remember?"

"About what?"

The doctor licked his lips. "What do you remember, from before you woke up here?"

Cyan considered this carefully. "Um. I'm...not sure?"

He cursed himself; his reply had come out as a question. But Dr Haven seemed satisfied. "It's normal to be confused. Fever can affect memory – even more so for someone under treatment here."

Cyan nodded slowly. "Ah. Yeah. I just remember normal stuff. Normal days. The usual blur."

"M-hm." Dr Haven took a thin silver torch from his coat and shone it briefly into each of Cyan's pupils before putting a cool hand to his forehead. "You're still warm. But I suspect you'll improve from here on. Ms Ferryman said she's fetching you some soup."

"Yeah. Turns out she's quite nice when you're on your deathbed. Usually she's a bit...grimmer." Cyan cringed. "But don't tell her I said that."

Dr Haven was washing his hands at a porcelain sink. "Sometimes there's more to a person than you think." He dried his hands and strolled to the door. "Keep eating and resting. You'll be back on your feet in no time."

Cyan watched the director leave. The moment the door closed, he pushed his forehead into his palms and breathed in long, shaking gasps.

First thing next morning, Cyan was out of medical quarters and back in uniform. He'd kept insisting he was fully recovered, until Ms Ferryman gave up protesting and told him – with her usual sternness restored – that he was welcome to leave and make himself ill again, if that's what he really wanted.

He got straight to work, searching the sanctuary and racing on his quad around the harbour and sands. And, as he'd expected, there was no trace of Jonquil.

Late that afternoon, while sitting with Teal and Ruby on the benches behind the sanctuary, Cyan glanced over his shoulder to make sure no one was listening in. Then he cleared his throat.

"That girl," he began, as casually as he could, "Jon-something. You know the one?"

Ruby's eyes didn't move from the book in her hand, but Teal turned his head. "Jon-who?"

"You know the one. Tall. Really long black hair. Brown skin. Fast runner. Always playing with her hands."

Teal pinched the tape on his glasses. "Jon-something…" His gaze drifted to the cove's mossy face. He shook his head. "Doesn't sound like anyone here."

He chewed on a fingernail. "Are you okay, Cyan? You're looking a bit flushed." His eyes widened and he shifted along the bench, trying to get some distance from Cyan. "Hang on… You still got some of that fever? Is it infectious?"

Cyan didn't answer. He'd checked again over his

shoulder and spotted an orderly looking at them through one of the sanctuary's windows.

Taking a book from his satchel, he pretended to read.

There was no doubt about it. Jonquil was gone and forgotten.

# BRUISING TO BLUE

The next day, Cyan raced full-throttle across the dunes. He had an appointment to keep.

He saw the whale bones ahead. Huge ribs pointed skywards, bearing the weight of a giant chain of vertebrae. And on top of the vertebrae was a silhouette: Ruby, with arms extended, hopping on one foot, crisp and bold against a paling sky.

Cyan's heart rate quickened at the sight, and he felt a prickling urge to get to her as swiftly as possible. He tried revving the quad harder but couldn't go faster.

While Ruby skipped down the slope of the whale's yellowing spine, Cyan rolled to a stop next to her quad. She was soon by his side, hopping gently with her plimsolls kicking left and right. "Ahoy, master of mystery! What kept you? Been waiting here for ages."

Cyan hung his goggles on his handlebar. "Thanks."

"*Be at the whale bones*," quoted Ruby, in a low, hammy voice. "*Alone. Tell no one.*" Her eyebrows jiggled while she laughed. "I didn't realize you'd turned into a cliché. What are you up to, whispering like a spy in the canteen?" She looked around suddenly, her eyes huge with exaggerated alarm. "Ooooh, are we being watched?"

"I hope not. Come on. Into the ribs."

Ruby skipped across sand and through the whale's parted jaws. Cyan followed slowly, scanning the sandscape as he moved. There was no sign of anyone. He saw only the distant mound of the cove; the twinkling rust of stranded ships; coarse tufts of beach grass; sand, sand and more sand.

Passing through the jaws, Cyan went straight to the rib he'd found the message on. He crouched and dug with his hands in the sand, but the etched letters were gone. He ran his fingers low along the rib, felt an area flatter and coarser than the rest of the bone. Someone had sanded the message away.

Ruby hitched her blue trousers a little, so she could sit with her arms wrapped around her legs. "What are you up to?"

"Looking for something."

"What?"

Cyan muttered and left the rib. "Something someone wanted gone."

He settled into a sandy groove across from Ruby and looked around again before speaking. "Teal didn't try to come along?"

Ruby seemed puzzled, but her smile soon returned. "I told him he looked under the weather. Said he might be getting that flu of yours. He got all worked up, like he was about to die or something. Went looking for Dr Haven."

Cyan's shoulders slumped. "A while ago I would have found that funny."

"It is funny. He's his own worst enemy. Does it to himself."

"But does he really?"

"What do you mean?"

Cyan didn't reply. Instead, he dug deep into his satchel and pulled out a handful of pills.

Ruby stared at them. "Is that mealtime medicine?"

Cyan nodded again.

"Why's it here?"

"I've been saving it up. In secret. I haven't taken any pills since I got out from medical quarters."

Ruby's mouth was as wide as it could go. "Are you out of your mind? What about… What about your treatment? You might…remember something!"

Cyan scooped a hole and started burying the pills. "Maybe remembering's not a bad thing."

"*What?*"

He saw Ruby shifting away from him, so that the base of her back stopped against a whale rib. Her hand moved to her pocket and Cyan held up his palm. "*Please*, Ruby. Don't use your locket. Just hear me out, okay? I need to show you something. If you want to call the orderlies after, go ahead. But let me show you first. It's something you really need to see."

Ruby's eyes were fixed on Cyan, though her hand continued slowly on its course.

"*Please*," repeated Cyan. He pushed his palms together. "I'm not going to talk about my past. I can't; I don't know anything about it. But I know about the present, and you need to know about it too."

Ruby's hand froze. "What do you mean, *the present*?" She peered around through pillars of bone. "Of course I know about the present."

"You think you do, but you don't." Cyan took a deep breath. "Please, Ruby. Just let me show you something. Then you can do what you want."

Ruby pushed her back further up the whale rib. She crossed her arms, and eyed Cyan for some time before finally speaking. "What is it you want to show me?"

Cyan cast his eyes east. "It's at the *Serenity*. We'll have to ride."

\* \* \*

After parking at the chasm's edge, Cyan and Ruby headed upwards through the *Serenity*'s engine rooms. Then they navigated corridors of mildewed carpet, until they were standing outside cabin 7270.

Cyan pointed through the doorway. "In there."

Ruby frowned at him before traipsing into the room. Her eyes searched the dank gloom, taking in the bed and its blanket of mould; the slanting drapes and rotting furniture.

"There," said Cyan. "The mirror."

Ruby approached the mirror on the dressing table. Cyan saw her frown deepen in its reflection, while she considered the four figures drawn with lipstick on the glass. He stood beside her, heard her murmuring.

"Me." She pointed at the cartoon with squiggles for hair. Her finger moved along the portraits. "And that's you. And there's Teal. And that…that…"

She lingered on the red sketch of Jonquil, with its narrow face and long, centre-parted hair. "Who's that?"

Cyan's words were hushed. "Her name's Jonquil."

Ruby's eyebrows drew together. "I don't know any Jonquil. Is she a new resident or something?"

"She's an old resident and she's a friend. *Your* friend."

Ruby puckered her lips, shook her head. "I don't know anyone called Jonquil."

"You do. You started these drawings on the mirror, and

**162**

we each drew our own portrait. Jonquil was here with us. She drew her own picture."

Ruby was squinting at the lipstick lines. "Nah. I've never been in this room. I didn't draw any of this."

"You've been made to forget. You had your memory of Jonquil removed – of all the time she was in the sanctuary. All the residents have. Apart from me."

Although Ruby scoffed, she stepped – with growing unease – away from the mirror. "You're making stuff up."

"I promise I'm not. Jonquil was a resident. We used to hang out. But something went wrong with her. The Lethe Method made her…ill. It's dangerous and it broke her. Dr Haven had everyone's memory of her wiped. So they'd carry on as normal, with no idea of how dangerous the treatment can be."

"That's stupid. The treatment's not dangerous."

"It is. It's not ready yet. It's an experiment. Dr Haven's using us – all the residents – as lab rats, to test and develop the method. Jonquil was a casualty, and everyone saw her have some sort of meltdown in the canteen. So the orderlies rounded everyone up. Knocked us all out so Dr Haven could remove our memories of her."

"Pfft." Ruby cocked her head. She was trying to smirk, but Cyan saw tautness in her cheeks, confusion in her eyes. "Okay, Mr Melodrama," she began. "If this is all true, why do *you* remember Jonquil? Why hasn't *your* memory been wiped?"

"Because I tricked Dr Haven. I woke up in... I don't know where it was. A room with white tiles. You and Teal were there, anaesthetized or sedated or whatever. Dr Haven let me wake up before removing my memories, so he could ask me some questions about Jonquil. He'd already interviewed you two.

"I got him out of the room, just long enough to swap the memory drug in his syringe with water. I think that's why I had a fever; maybe injecting the water made me ill. But I remember everything: what Dr Haven said about the treatment; how he took Jonquil away."

Ruby broke into a sneer. "Can you hear yourself, Cyan? You sound like you've lost your mind."

"You think so?"

"Yeah, I do."

Cyan nodded at Ruby's trouser pocket. "Then why haven't you called the sanctuary?"

"I..." Ruby's mouth hung open. Closing it, she turned her face to the mirror.

Cyan followed her gaze, so that he was looking at Jonquil's outline too. "You're not sure. I can tell. You remember her, don't you."

Ruby didn't reply.

"Don't you?"

A gradual shake of the head. "No. I don't. I don't remember her at all." Ruby's mouth tightened. "But this picture, and the way you talk about her... Something about the name..." The shoulders of her blazer sagged. "It makes me...*feel* something."

"Like what?"

"Sort of...sad. And weirdly worried. Or something like that. I'm not sure. But it doesn't feel good."

Cyan nodded to himself. He spoke gently. "Emotional residue."

Ruby's eyes were on him. "Emotional what?"

"Residue. Dregs. Sort of...the emotional stuff left over from what's been forgotten. The treatment can't get rid of it; it can only bury it. From what Dr Haven said, having it build up without knowing it's there does the damage – the damage that made Jonquil fall to pieces. That's why the treatment's dangerous. That's what Dr Haven's trying to fix, but with all of us as his lab rats."

Ruby was staring again at Jonquil's empty outline. She began to shake her head. "No. This can't be right." Cyan heard the tremble in her voice. "You're making all this up. Trying to freak me out."

"There's more."

Cyan went to the bedside table. He opened its drawer and was relieved to find the message still etched inside; Dr Haven must have failed to figure out the bone code.

He beckoned Ruby over and moved aside so she could read.

*Between green and red*

*Me: Ruth McMurphy*

*Mum: Helen McMurphy, blonde pixie hair, blue-grey eyes, best cuddles ever, smells like fresh soil in the garden, sings quietly in the bath*

*Dad: James McMurphy, bald shiny head, nerdy glasses, tickly black beard, brown eyes, Santa belly laugh, terrible jokes, smells like baking*

*Brother: Ben McMurphy, scoundrel, long blond curls, massive blue eyes, cute nose, noisy and lovely and smells like malty milk*

*Home: Nottingham in England, by the horse field in Bestwood*

*Best to deceive the memory thieves*

*Fight don't forget, hold on or it's gone*

Ruby took a cautious step backwards while she read, as if afraid of the drawer's contents. "What…"

"I found it here the day we drew ourselves on the mirror. There was a code on the whale bones that led me here. It's been removed now. Just like Jonquil."

"But what is this?" Ruby inched forward again, craning her neck towards the drawer.

"I think it's a resident who was trying to keep hold of her memories. Someone who was fighting the treatment."

Ruby's hand rose to her lips. "God… This Ruth

McMurphy…" Her voice was still unsteady. "She might be someone we know."

"Probably forgotten all this by now. That's my guess. But maybe not."

"What does 'between green and red' mean?"

"I still haven't figured that out. But if this Ruth was fighting the treatment, I'm guessing she had doubts. Maybe she sensed it was dangerous. Or maybe she found out Dr Haven's up to no good."

Some of the trembling left Ruby's voice. "This is all guesswork." She peered at Jonquil's outline. "I… I still don't know what to make of it all."

"But you know the treatment's flawed. You know you're not as well as you should be."

Ruby looked puzzled. Her eyes went to Cyan again. "Do I?"

"Your sadness. The emptiness that…pins you like a bug."

Some of the colour left Ruby's face. Cyan flinched. She looked so wounded.

"How…" she began. Her voice was brittle, but her eyes narrowed coldly. "Who told you about that?"

"You did. One night a while ago, when you showed me how to get into the framework."

Ruby gaped at Cyan. Her fingers clenched and curled. "I've…*never* shown you that. I never would!"

"You did, Ruby. I swear. And you told me about the

loneliness you get sometimes. The feelings Dr Haven tells you to keep secret. And I told you about my fear – how I'm scared of fire, and how Dr Haven tells me to keep that secret too."

"But I don't remember any of this! I—" Ruby's lips twisted with words she couldn't find.

Cyan saw her chest heaving, put a gentle hand on her arm. He spoke steadily and calmly. "That's because it all happened while Jonquil was around." He nodded towards the mirror. "Do you see the proof now, Ruby? Dr Haven's removed *everyone's* memories. To keep the danger here hidden."

It took a while for Ruby to speak again. She stared at the outlines on the mirror. The breaths that heaved through her nose began to level.

When she spoke, her words were hoarse. "We need to tell someone about this."

Cyan sighed. "I know. But who are we supposed to tell?" He ruffled his hair with both hands. "If we tell the staff, we'll be taken to Dr Haven to have everything we know removed. And then we'll be in danger again, without even knowing it. There'll be no chance of helping Jonquil 'cos no one'll know she exists. It'd be back to square one. Square zero, even."

Ruby's eyes roved the cabin. "What about the other residents?"

"I thought about that. But if we told any residents, what'd happen then? They might not believe me; you nearly didn't. And even if they did, it'd be the canteen all over again. We'd be rounded up and knocked out, and then we'd have all the memories removed. Dr Haven presses the reset button, and again we're back at square zero. Lab rats in ignorant bliss."

Ruby gave this some thought. She pressed two fingers against her lips, then narrowed her eyes at Cyan. "But you told me. Why?"

Cyan wasn't sure what to say. He met Ruby's gaze, and sucked in some air before replying. "Because I'm scared, Ruby. I had to tell *someone*."

He looked ruefully at the tall outline on the mirror. "And I need to find Jonquil. I feel like I…put her at risk. I sent her to Dr Haven when she tried to talk about her past. She was never the same after that. I need to find her and help her. But I can't do it alone so…I was hoping you might…help me. You were her friend."

Ruby gestured at the plumper figure on the glass. "Teal's her friend too, right? You could have asked him for help."

One of Cyan's eyebrows rose. "Teal can barely cope with itchy shirts, Ruby, let alone this. And he's not great under pressure. You should have seen him when they sent the helicopter to get Jonquil."

"Helicopter?"

"That was when she tried to open up to us. Before Dr Haven gave her extra treatment." Cyan grimaced and pushed his fingers through his hair. "But what I'm saying is…we can't let Teal know about *any* of this. Dr Haven said his worrying comes from all the repressed emotion that hurts residents; he's more vulnerable than you think. I wouldn't want to force this on him. Plus…" He trailed off and felt his cheeks flush with warmth. "Telling you just feels sort of…*right*. Do you know what I mean?"

Ruby looked mystified. She flicked a spiral of hair from her eyes. "No. I don't."

"Either way, will you help me?"

Ruby chewed gloomily at her lower lip. "Help you to do what, though, Cyan? What can we actually do about this?"

"I haven't figured that out yet. But I know Jonquil's in trouble. And it feels like the longer we leave it, the more trouble she'll be in. If we can find her we can hide her somewhere safe, until we think of something. Maybe we can even reach the shore with her, flag down a boat or something. Whatever we manage to do, it's got to be better than leaving her at the sanctuary with Dr Haven."

"Do you even know she's still at the sanctuary?"

"Dr Haven said he was keeping her there for more research – not far from wherever that room with the white tiles is. Before I passed out I heard him tell Mr Banter to get my file from next door. I think Jonquil must be on the staff floor somewhere."

A sideward glance from Ruby. "We can't get down there. You need staff cards."

"Yeah, but there might be another way. We can get to the engine floor through the framework. You said you think it has access to the staff floor. So I'm thinking we sneak down tonight, when everyone's asleep. Have a look and go from there."

Ruby scrunched up her face. "I don't know, Cyan. That's a really iffy plan."

"Probably. But it's all we have. Unless you've got any better ideas?"

Cyan could see from her expression that she didn't.

He stared down at the mouldy carpet, before sheepishly raising his eyes. "So…will you help me?"

Ruby met his gaze before turning to the mirror and letting out a long, sorry sigh. "I don't think we have any choice. No one else can help Jonquil, can they?"

The pair fell silent, until muffled beeps had them reaching for their pockets. While unclipping his locket, Cyan glanced at the window. The sky above the chasm had bruised to blue. He checked his locket's screen. "Lunchtime."

Ruby nodded, pocketed her locket and went glumly to the door. "So what's it like?"

Cyan followed her into the corridor. "What's what like?"

"Being off the pills."

"I'm…not sure." Cyan gave this some thought while they headed to the engine rooms. "It's only been two or three days. But I feel sort of…sharper."

"Sharper?"

"Yeah. Everything feels sharper."

"As in…it hurts?"

"No. As in focus. I feel…a bit clearer now. Less…fuzzy. And it's not just that…"

Cyan thought about the way his heart had raced when he'd spotted Ruby earlier, but decided against mentioning it. "It's intense too. All my feelings are stronger. As if they're under a magnifying glass. Like being alone or afraid… I'm more scared now than I've ever been before. As far as I can remember, at least."

He clenched his eyes shut, then kicked a stray, mould-encrusted suitcase along the corridor. "So, yeah. It's intense. But at least if I avoid the medication, there's less chance of whatever happened to Jonquil happening to me."

"That's the theory."

"Yeah." Cyan caught up with Ruby. "What about you?"

"What about me?"

"Will you be skipping your medicine too?"

Ruby shook her head. "I think I'll see how it works out for you first. You can be my guinea pig."

Cyan grunted and shoved his hands into his pockets. "Looks like we're all guinea pigs anyway."

# DEEPER

Late that night – or perhaps in the black, early hours of morning – Cyan clambered through a snug's opening into a dimly lit shaft. Rather than climbing up towards dune-light, he inhaled a large gulp of oily air and began heading down the ladder. The engine floor waited beneath him, deep in the darkness below.

He didn't know how long he'd been climbing; only that his thighs and forearms ached to the point of burning. His hands smelled metallic from gripping an endless row of rungs.

After more climbing, Cyan glanced down and saw – with a queasy clash of relief and dread – that the shaft ended not far beneath his feet. He peered about the gloom. The final horizontal shaft was just above his head. Below him the ladder entered dim, empty air.

Cyan descended further, freed one hand from a rung

and tipped himself towards the opening. He saw the shaft's four ladders meet a network of gangways, between which sat huge machines and clusters of cogs, all aglimmer in the glow of muted lights.

He listened out and surveyed the area. The coast seemed clear so – as silently as he could – he slipped down the ladder and crouched behind a generator.

He'd been squatting for some time, trying to figure out what to do next, when a shifting shadow made him start. A face appeared at the corner and muttered a deadpan, "Boo."

"*Sshhhh*," hissed Cyan. He glanced around frantically, with his tingling fingers gripping the gangway.

"It's okay," whispered Ruby. "No one's around. Been dead since I got here."

Cyan wiped his forehead, which felt hot and clammy in the cool air. "Do you know where to go? You said there's stairs to the staff floor."

"A lift too. They're at opposite sides. Must be the lift and stairs the restricted-access doors near the foyer go to. I'm guessing they go down to the staff floor."

"Let's hope so." Cyan cocked an ear to check for sounds of anyone else. All was quiet, so he went on. "From what I've seen from the foyer, the staff use the lift pretty much every time. So let's try the stairs. Less risk."

Keeping low, Cyan followed Ruby past mammoth cogs,

silent engines, oiled pistons, cables and pulleys. He saw two wooden columns among the ladders that dropped from above, each containing a staircase that led from the foyer to the upper rooms.

When they reached the far wall, Ruby opened a heavy grey door. Behind it was a drab stairwell, with concrete walls and steps of metal mesh.

She grimaced wryly at Cyan. "Going down."

Tiptoeing down the U-shaped staircase, they paused by a door with *FLOOR 2: COMMUNAL* stencilled above its top, then continued down to the final floor, where a door labelled *FLOOR 1: STAFF* awaited them.

Cyan whispered in dim grey light. "This is it."

Ruby nodded gravely. "What now?"

"We take a peek."

Cyan stooped and shuffled to the door, then raised his eyes to the small window at its top. The light on the other side was murky, so he had to press his nose and spectacles to the glass.

Ruby was staring from the door frame, bobbing nervously on her feet. "What can you see?" she hissed.

"Good news and bad news. The good news is there's no one around. Seems quiet. There's dimmed lighting too, like in here. So we can see where we're going. But maybe any light is bad news. I'm not sure."

"What's the bad news you *are* sure about?"

"It's a really long corridor. Leads right to the lift at the opposite side. And there's several doors along the way, all spread out."

"Why's that bad?"

"Means there's lots down here to search through. Which means more risk of getting caught. The staff sleep here, remember. Someone could turn up. And if they do, there's not much in the corridor for hiding. Just a few trolleys."

"Oh."

They lingered by the door. Cyan rubbed his chin and pushed his glasses up his nose. Ruby stared at the concrete floor, and stopped jiggling her knee when she saw Cyan frowning at her.

He nodded to himself. "Okay. I say we take a side each. I'll check the doors along the left; you take the ones on the right. Just peeking in, as quick as we can. This is a scouting operation for now – unless you see Jonquil. Then we meet straight back here and share our intel. Figure out our next move."

Ruby sniggered.

Cyan's white eyebrows drew together. "What?"

"*Intel*," she mimicked. "Since when did you become a secret agent?"

Cyan scowled. "Are you taking this seriously? Do you know what'll happen if we're caught sneaking around? We'll get our memories erased, and then Jonquil's gone for ever. And who knows what else Dr Haven might do to us. I've seen his true colours now, and they're pretty dark."

Ruby scratched sheepishly at the back of her neck. "Sorry, Cyan. But it… I'm just…*really* scared. It's nerves, I guess. You know what I mean?"

Cyan gazed at his plimsolls before raising his eyes again. "Yeah. I know what you mean." He straightened his back and inhaled deeply through his mouth. When he released his breath it came out shakier than he'd hoped. "Okay. Let's do this. I'll take the doors on the left. You take the ones on the right. Quick and quiet."

"Like stealthy cats."

Ruby tried to smile, but Cyan could see the strain in her expression. He tried to smile too. "Yeah. Like stealthy cats. In slippers."

"That went to ninja school."

They both smiled then, until Cyan put his hand to the door.

After leaving the safety of the stairwell, Cyan and Ruby crept to the first doors on each side of the corridor.

The door to the left had a brass nameplate: *Professor Vadasz, Technical Manager*. Cyan eased it open, just enough to squint through the crack.

The office was empty and lit by nothing more than the

large computer monitor on the professor's desk. The image on the screen looked familiar. When Cyan realized what it was, he leaned back into the corridor. "Psst."

Ruby turned from her own doorway and let Cyan usher her into the professor's office.

He whispered after shutting the door. "What was in your room?"

"It's a massive storage space. The lights were dimmed, so I couldn't see right to the back. But it was furniture, mostly. Shelves and racks with pictures and light fittings and stuff."

"It's what they use for changing the rooms."

Ruby rolled her eyes. "Good work, Sherlock." She scanned the cables and equipment on the professor's shelves. "What's this room?"

"Professor Vadasz's office. Check this out."

Cyan beckoned her to the computer on the desk. They studied the cube-shaped grid on its flickering screen.

"It's the sanctuary," whispered Cyan. "A 3-D map." His finger worked its way up from the cube's base. Staff floor; communal floor; engine floor. And the upper rooms."

Ruby ran a fingernail between the dots scattered across the grid. "And look. These have all got residents' names next to them. Must be where all the residents are. This computer's tracking lockets."

She squinted in the screen's light. Her finger zipped to

a dot labelled *Ruby*. "There's mine. By BF3. That's where I climbed in through the snug."

Cyan searched the screen, and his finger shot up towards another dot. "That's mine. DH9. No wonder it took so long to get down."

Ruby was still searching the screen. "I can't see a dot for Jonquil."

"I doubt she's got a locket now. And have you noticed? There's no dots for staff either. Staff lockets aren't tracked."

Ruby's eyes roved across pixels. "Yeah. You're right." She glanced over her shoulder at the office door. "Come on. Let's try the other rooms. The sooner we're done with this the better."

While Ruby progressed along the corridor's right side, Cyan moved on to the next room on the left. Using a torch he'd found in a socket by its door, he peered inside and searched the darkness. It was a larger room, with blueprints covering the walls and boiler suits hanging up in rows; presumably the technicians' room.

The next room along was even bigger, with coffee tables and communal seating. Cyan flashed his torch through the doorway, guessing from some stacked white uniforms that this was the orderlies' staffroom. He was about to move on when his beam crossed a filing cabinet by the wall.

Cyan hesitated. And then, with thoughts of what Dr Haven had said about his file – with thoughts, even, of what the doctor had said about his parents – he let himself in.

The cabinet was filled with order forms and paperwork; no residents' files.

Cyan sighed and slid the cabinet's drawer shut. His heart felt heavy in his chest, and he realized with some sadness how high his hopes had been – how eager he'd been to learn about his parents.

His torch threw a white circle along the walls, flitting like a moth across noticeboards prickled with pins; posters of maritime scenes; plug sockets and shelves; whiteboards smeared with ink.

Another metal cabinet – this one much taller than the first – caught Cyan's eye. Again, he was unable to resist. He opened its double doors, and instead of files found stacks of white plastic cartridges.

"Ahoy, pointy tranquilizers. Don't mind if I do." While slipping a cartridge into his blazer pocket, he spotted a tray on another shelf filled with staff access cards. "And ahoy to you too," he whispered, pocketing a card for good measure.

He closed the cabinet and moved on, but stopped when his torchlight met a pinboard spanning a huge section of wall. The torch's white circle moved slowly up, down and across, pausing on some of the sheets that were pinned to the board.

"What?" Cyan stepped closer.

There must have been over a hundred sheets, all lined up in tidy columns. Cyan's beam moved frantically, illuminating photos of residents. He saw a picture of Teal, then moved backwards along the alphabet to find one of Ruby.

Every sheet had text next to its photo. Cyan began to read Ruby's but stopped. Not only because it felt wrong, but because something was dawning on him.

Again, his torchlight searched the sheets. He paused on some for longer than others, then finally understood. Among the pictures were photos of other residents – residents he didn't recognize at all.

His beam passed a face he hadn't seen in some time, then flitted back again.

And there she was. That tidy centre parting. Those high cheekbones. The sorrow in those deep brown eyes.

Jonquil.

And stamped in red letters across the text by her face: *WITHDRAWN*

Cyan stopped breathing. He continued skimming the sheets with his torch and began to see a pattern: all the residents he didn't recognize had *WITHDRAWN* stamped on them too.

"But…" he croaked. "But that—"

He fell silent when his light found another red-stamped

resident, with pale skin and a blonde bob of hair. He read her name again, and found himself thinking of whale bones – of notes in drawers and green and red…

"Amber," he whispered.

# WITHDRAWN

Cyan didn't realize he was backing away until something hard met his calf. It was too late to stop, and his retreat became a stumble that sent his torchlight soaring across the ceiling. He'd been tripped by a low coffee table, and even though he managed to stagger sideways before hitting the floor, a stack of glasses was left teetering on the table's top.

Cyan aimed his torch at the glasses, just in time to watch them topple and crash against a water jug.

The noise was obscene: a storm of glass against glass.

With his stomach cramping, Cyan flicked off the torch. Darkness fell and he held his breath. Heat bloomed across his cheeks and palms.

The passing seconds stretched and coiled, until the silence was broken again. A door, opening and closing in the corridor.

Cyan mouthed a silent curse. The gloom lifted by a hue and he saw that the thin line beneath the door was brighter. Someone had switched on the corridor lights.

The clop of shoes sent him scrabbling on hands and knees across the floor. He took cover behind a bench that curved in an L-shape around the coffee table. His breaths came short and shallow, and he threw a hand over his mouth when the staffroom door opened.

The door closed. A quiet click flooded the room with light.

Cyan squinted through the gap between the floor and the bench's base. He could see two shoes by the door, beneath the stiff hems of white trousers. It was an orderly.

Staying as still and quiet as he could, Cyan watched while the shoes moved slowly through the room, following the wall, drawing closer to the coffee table and bench. His stomach tightened with each kick of his heart. The orderly was almost upon him.

He was on the cusp of crying out when something stopped the shoes in their tracks: a dull thump against the wall, from the next room along.

The shoes pivoted and went back the way they'd come. The moment the door closed, Cyan collapsed sideways onto the floor. He was gasping for air when he realized where the orderly was heading.

"*Ruby!*" he breathed, scrabbling to his feet. Moving

lightly on his plimsolls, he followed the orderly's path to the door, eased the handle down and peeked into the corridor. There was no sign of anyone, but when he leaned further through the doorway, he caught sight of the next door along closing.

His hands flew into his hair. After clenching his eyes shut, he nodded to himself, stepped into the corridor and began tiptoeing towards the door.

"Psst."

The sound came from behind. Cyan spun on his feet and saw Ruby pop up behind a trolley stacked with uniforms. His mouth fell open and he jerked his thumb towards the door.

"*Orderly!*" he mouthed. "*In there!*"

"*I know!*" mouthed Ruby in return. "*Let's go!*" She gestured wildly towards the door to the stairwell.

Half-creeping, half-dashing, Cyan joined her in a scurry for the stairwell, but was startled when someone clutched the hem of his blazer.

He twisted with his arms flying up and saw with some confusion that it was Ruby who'd grabbed him. She snatched the torch from his hand and slotted it carefully into its socket by the technician's room. Cyan's mouth formed an O, and they continued on their run, until they were out of the corridor and up the stairs.

\* \* \*

186

The pair of them panted together, crouched between cogs on the engine floor.

Ruby flicked some curls stuck with sweat to her forehead. "Did…" she puffed, but she had to stop. She put a hand to her chest and took deep breaths. "The orderly – did he see you?"

Cyan shook his head. "No. Was close, though. *Really* close. A noise from next door made him leave." He wiped the side of his hand across his upper lip. "What was that? The thump – I thought it must be you. But you were in the corridor."

"It *was* me. I went looking for you in the last room on your side when I heard something smash, and then the light went on in the corridor. Then I heard someone go to the room the noise came from, but it stayed quiet, so I figured you'd broken something and were hiding. I banged the wall – you know, to create a distraction – then ran out and hid behind the trolley. Thought the orderly might investigate the noise – give us a chance to get away."

Cyan stared at her and puffed up his cheeks. "Man alive, Ruby. You're a genius." Wincing, he bowed and shook his head. "I messed up, though. It'll be hard to search the staff floor again. They'll be on their guard now."

Ruby's eyebrows sank. "So what was that noise? *Did* you break something?"

"Tripped on a coffee table. Knocked over a stack of glasses."

Ruby looked appalled. "What happened to stealthy ninja cat?"

"Ninja cat got a shock."

"A shock?"

"I saw something in the orderlies' staffroom. There were sheets on a board, one for each resident, with photos, personality profiles, behavioural tendencies – stuff like that."

"What?" Ruby glanced down and up again. "Did you see mine?"

"I did. But reading it felt…like prying, I guess. And I was more interested in Jonquil's sheet. No offence."

Ruby's eyes widened. "There was one for Jonquil?"

"Yeah. With a red stamp on it that said *WITHDRAWN*, in big capital letters. But she wasn't the only one."

"How do you mean?"

Cyan screwed his eyes shut. "There were *loads* of them, Ruby. Loads of residents with *WITHDRAWN* stamped on them. At least twenty. And apart from Jonquil, I didn't recognize any of them."

Ruby shuffled closer. She was barely breathing. "Wait… Are you saying…"

Cyan nodded. "Yeah. Jonquil's not the only one. There're loads of residents who've been removed from the sanctuary and from our memories. Probably because they've all been hurt by the treatment, just like Jonquil.

More of Dr Haven's casualties."

Ruby's gaze drifted to the metal gangway. "Oh my god."

"And one of them was called *Amber*," continued Cyan. "I think she might be Ruth – the one who left that message in the *Serenity* and on the bones."

Ruby's eyes shot back up. "Amber? As in…like, traffic lights?"

"Yeah. Between green and red. So Amber – I mean, Ruth – she's one of the residents who've been hurt and removed from our memories."

Ruby's hand was over her mouth. "This is big, Cyan. Like, *really* big."

"I know." Cyan tapped her other hand. "What about you? Did you find anything? Any sign of Jonquil or…or anyone else?"

Ruby shook her head.

"What about the room with white tiles? Was that on your side?"

"I didn't see anything like that. After the first room there was just a laundry room and then a massive food larder. The last room was some sort of living space, with sofas and tables and stuff, and loads more doors around the edges."

Cyan looked sideways while visualizing. "The staff's living quarters. Those doors lead to their bedrooms. You can see them through the windows outside."

"That's what I thought. And the last room on your side, where I knocked on the wall – that was just pipes and boilers. I peeked into the lift as well. It's massive, but nothing unusual. I don't—"

Something stopped her: the dull echo of shoes on concrete, coming from the doorway to the stairwell.

"Someone's coming!" hissed Ruby.

Cyan was already on his feet. "Meet me at the whale bones! Tomorrow!"

They turned from each other and fled in opposite directions. Cyan ducked past gangways to reach his ladder, and soon found shelter in a darkened shaft.

# LAST ONE WHERE

"Mum! Dad!"

Cyan woke and sat bolt upright in his bed. He put a trembling hand to his throat, which felt sore from the scream just torn from his lungs.

He looked groggily from left to right, taking in the book on his bedside table; the potted sea holly on the shelves; the fluffy beanbag and bright orange lamp; the room's frame with its four shadowy snugs.

Cyan wondered where the cry had come from – had he been dreaming? – and whispered hoarsely to no one. "Mum?"

A rush of heat prickled his eyelids, burning so fiercely he had to shut his eyes and push his palms against them. While they were closed, Cyan shivered on the bed and tried to remember something – anything at all – about his parents. He squeezed his eyes shut even harder, willing something to come to him, searching the darkness behind his eyelids.

But there was nothing. No hint of a voice, no trace of a face. No scent or softness, no warmth nor touch.

Nothing except the dry sting of his eyes.

Still trembling, Cyan collapsed back onto the mattress, pulled the pillow from beneath his head and hugged it as tightly as he could.

Cyan had no appetite but – in an attempt to look normal and avoid suspicion – he got dressed and plodded to the canteen when his locket called him for breakfast.

There was no sign of Ruby or Teal; they must have got different breakfast shifts. So Cyan sat alone and played with his cereal, being sure to check no one was looking when he palmed the morning's pills into his satchel.

He was keen to get to the whale bones to meet Ruby, so after a short while he left the canteen, crossed the foyer and hit the marble steps beyond the revolving door. He was about to break into a run, but faltered when someone called his name.

He followed the sound and saw Teal getting up from the bottom step. "Ahoy, Teal."

Teal brushed sand from his hands. "Where were you yesterday? Couldn't find you anywhere. Ruby neither."

"Er…"

"What d'you fancy doing today?"

Cyan winced and rubbed the back of his neck. "I can't hang around, Teal. Got some…stuff to do."

Teal headed up the steps towards him. "Stuff? What stuff? You want me to help out?"

Cyan chewed his bottom lip. "Actually, it's better if… I just… I need to…" The more Cyan mumbled and rubbed his neck, the more Teal's eyebrows sank.

"Why're you making excuses? You don't what to hang out?"

"It's not like that. More like…"

Teal shoved his hands into his blazer pockets. "Are you going to see Ruby? Were you with each other yesterday?"

"Um… Maybe?"

"What were you doing?"

"Nothing."

Teal was nodding sternly. "Nothing, but something you want me left out of, right?"

Cyan held his palms up, cringing. "We're not leaving you out of anything, I promise. We'll hang out later, yeah?"

Teal shrugged. "Maybe I don't want to. Maybe you guys don't deserve Teal time."

Cyan couldn't resist a slight smile. "Teal time? Is that what you call it?"

"Smirk all you want, Cyan, but you're the one missing

193

out. So go on." He wafted Cyan away like a bad smell. "Off you go. You've got *stuff* to do."

After throwing Teal a pained look, Cyan touched his arm and darted down the steps. He turned and jogged backwards to face him. "I'll make it up to you! I promise!"

Even from a distance, Cyan could see Teal's surly expression waning. He had no doubt that a thousand anxieties were passing through his friend's mind. Cursing himself, he turned away and continued towards the hangar, keen to find a quad that would get him to the bones.

A little later, Cyan sat alone between strips of shadow. He stared out from behind mammoth ribs, scanning the sandscape for signs of movement. Eventually he clocked a quad crossing the dunes, heading in his direction, closing in quick. Brown curls caught the sun, and Cyan's fists stopped their clenching.

He'd been waiting at the bones for about an hour.

An hour?

His eyebrows rose. Cyan felt strangely sure of how much time had passed. He looked up and winced at the sun, which had made some headway along its daily arc. He studied the brightening blue of the sky, then lowered his gaze to watch the dunes' shrinking shadows.

Yes. About an hour.

"Ahoy." Ruby waved half-heartedly from her quad, hung up her goggles and crossed some beach grass.

"Ahoy."

As she passed through gaping jaws of bone, Cyan pondered the sour, determined look on her face. Where did Ruby get it from – all that spirit and fire? Thinking back to what she'd told him in the framework, he wondered whether it was something to do with the feelings of abandonment she'd mentioned. Some sort of balance or reaction. Or maybe it came from her upbringing. From her mum and dad.

Cyan was overcome by a sudden, almost painful urge to ask Ruby about her past. He ached to know what her parents did for a living, what they were like as people. But he realized immediately that asking would be pointless. Ruby knew as much about her old life as he did about his: absolutely nothing at all.

She stopped in front of him, dropped her satchel and brushed sand from her lapel. Today's uniform was black. "How you holding up?"

A listless doff of Cyan's imaginary cap. "Shipshape. And you?"

Ruby shrugged. "Not great. Turns out ignorance really is bliss."

"Don't be fooled. Ignorance is dangerous."

Ruby perched herself beside her satchel. While crossing her legs, she reached into her pocket and pulled out some pills.

Cyan watched her bury them in sand. "You're dodging your doses too?"

Ruby smoothed the sand over. "There're twenty-odd residents somewhere who've been horribly damaged by the treatment, hidden away and wiped from our memories. Makes sense to cut back on the medicine."

"Agreed."

"Has anyone talked to you today?"

"Not beyond the usual ahoys and pleasantries. What about you? Has anyone mentioned last night?"

"Not yet."

"I guess that's something."

Ruby frowned uneasily. "I guess so." She drummed her fingers against a jittery knee. "We're going to need help, aren't we."

"Obviously. But who's going to help us?"

Ruby gazed in the sanctuary's direction. "Do you think we should tell Teal after all?"

Cyan thought about his recent encounter with Teal on the steps. He sighed and shook his head. "No. I mean, I *hate* leaving him out, but getting him involved is too risky. I told you what Dr Haven said about him. Telling him about the danger he's in could tip him over the edge. I don't want to see any more friends go through what Jonquil went through."

Ruby gave this some thought, then began to nod. "Fair enough."

"So we're back to the same question. Who's going to help us?"

Ruby rubbed her nose. She was looking between the bones now, with her eyesk fixed to the south. "Whoever we can find. This is too big for us to handle alone." She pointed through the ribs. "I say we head that way and keep going."

"But there's nothing out there, Ruby. Just more sand. You can see it all from the top of the *Serenity*."

"So let's go further. We've never kept going before. There was never any reason to. But now there is. And there's got to be someone. There's got to be *something*. That's the way the hovercraft comes in. The helicopter too."

Cyan followed Ruby's gaze, then lifted his eyes to the clouds, which hung like grey blimps over the dunes.

"What do you think?" asked Ruby.

Cyan got up and clapped sand from his trousers. He headed for the quads. "I think we've got nothing to lose."

When they'd both snapped on their goggles, Ruby called out over the hum of engines. "Last one there's a rotten egg?"

Both quads snarled in chorus.

"Last one where?" shouted Cyan.

Ruby nodded at the horizon. "I guess we'll find out!" She yanked the throttle and her quad surged ahead.

\* \* \*

What started as a race soon became a slog; a marathon with a finish line Cyan wasn't sure existed.

On and on they went, throttles at full tilt, the roars of two engines reduced to an endless drone. The tilted, towering *Serenity* dwindled in their wake, smaller than it had ever been before. They'd never been so far out on the sands. This was new territory.

And yet it wasn't. On and on they went, wordless and grim. The only thing that changed was the sky above their heads. Clouds gathered and the air began to dim. The sands remained the same, unfolding towards a horizon that was eternally unmoving, endlessly unbroken.

Cyan knew he was moving, and at decent speed. Rusting shipwrecks approached and flew by. The bones of large fish crunched beneath his tyres. His blazer flapped and flailed, and airborne grit caught in his nostrils and teeth. But he felt motionless. The horizon remained where it was, no matter how straight and fast he went. He was stuck on a treadmill of dunes, moving quickly but bound for nowhere.

Glancing across at Ruby, Cyan could see she felt the same. Her russet hair writhed around her goggles, whipping a face that looked more bored than resolved.

And then, as one and without warning, the quad bikes slowed down.

Cyan and Ruby exchanged looks. They checked their fuel gauges, released their handles, then revved again. But the quads continued to decelerate. Their engines spluttered, and both bikes – without any say-so from their riders – rolled to a stop.

They were stranded on the sands.

# SOMETIME-SOMEWHERE

Ruby pulled uselessly at her throttle. "What happened?" She tapped her fuel gauge. "My tank's still half-full."

"Mine too."

They sat in silence, checking their quads' dashboards. Cyan looked up towards the horizon, then twisted on his seat to squint in the direction from which they'd come.

Raindrops began to patter his face. A wave of tiredness rushed in and he felt an urge to lie forward against his quad – to close his eyes and never open them again. But the feeling went as quickly as it came, washed away by thoughts of Jonquil, Amber and all the others.

He massaged his neck, which still ached from the cry that had left his throat that morning, and felt some strength returning.

"Hang on," he said, climbing off his seat. Heaving from the front, he pushed the quad back along the tracks it had churned in the sand. Then he climbed on and tried the ignition. The engine trembled and broke into a steady purr.

Easing the throttle, Cyan edged the quad slowly forward. As soon as it neared Ruby's, the engine clicked off and the bike stopped again. He shrugged at Ruby and gazed north. "You know what this means, don't you?"

Ruby followed his gaze, back in the direction of the sanctuary. "The quads have got limited range. They're programmed to turn off at a certain point."

"Bullseye. Someone doesn't want residents going out too far."

Ruby nodded slowly. The raindrops thickened. "So what do we do?"

"There's only two choices. We continue on foot, or we turn back."

Ruby peered at the dunes rolling southward to the skyline. "Sounds more like one choice to me. There's still nothing out there. Nothing we can see or reach by foot, anyway."

A sigh left Cyan's mouth. "Yeah. We'd better turn round, head back."

"Then what?"

"Back to the original plan. We find Jonquil ourselves. And hopefully the others too."

Ruby's expression was almost a sneer. "Are you serious?" She threw an arm towards the emptiness ahead. "Even if we found them, there's nowhere to take them."

"But finding them would be a start, right? We can't just leave them. And if we find them…" Cyan's lips moved with his thoughts. "If we find them, they'll be proof to the other residents of what Dr Haven's doing. That way, if the orderlies start whipping their tranquilizers out, the residents might put up a fight. Plus we'd have the residents we've rescued on our side."

"Assuming they're capable of doing anything. Or that they're even alive."

Cyan couldn't bring himself to think about that. He went on, his words coming more rapidly. "And if we find the hidden residents, maybe we can find more tranquilizer needles too. We can use them against the orderlies. Maybe we can force them to take us all off the island. On the hovercraft. To somewhere safe."

Ruby gawped at him through the falling drizzle. "Have you lost your tiny mind, Cyan? That's a *huge* pile of ifs and maybes. Is that what you call a plan?"

Cyan hesitated. "I…think so?"

"That's not a plan at all. It's an idiot's deluded fantasy."

Cyan's hands were in the air. "Then what else are we supposed to do? Go back to the sanctuary and pretend nothing ever happened? Take pills and ask Dr Haven to remove our memories, so we can be happy little lab rats again?"

Ruby glared at him. "Actually, right now forgetting doesn't sound all that bad. Things were better before."

"*Were they really?*" Cyan caught himself scowling. He closed his eyes, put his palms to his face and gulped down salty air. When he lowered his hands, he saw that Ruby's expression had changed. She looked as frightened as he felt.

He reached across from his quad, put his hand on hers. "Ruby. I'm sorry. I get what you're saying. I honestly do. Things felt better, but they weren't really, were they? Going by the number of residents Dr Haven's removed, I'd say we're all just ticking timebombs, on our way to exploding because of all the stuff we're holding in. We're forgetting and we're evading and it's *hurting* us. So, I don't know about you, Ruby, but I'm done with forgetting."

Spreading his arms, Cyan twisted on his bike to gesture in a semi-circle. "I'm done with this island. I mean, look around! There's nothing here. It's all just sand and salt and bones. I know what Jonquil meant now."

"Meant by what?"

"It was by the *Serenity*, just before I…" Cyan grimaced and shook his head. "Before I had her dragged away by Mr Banter. She talked about how there's no life here on the island; no birds or bugs or animals. No nothing. I used to sense it, I think, but was able to ignore it. But not now. Not since I stopped the pills. This place is…dead."

Ruby stared blankly at her knee, which was jiggling against her quad bike's side. "It's not *all* bad, Cyan. We've had…fun here." Her knee stopped and she pouted darkly. "Had."

Cyan wiped some raindrops from his glasses. "I don't think it was really ever fun, Ruby. It was just…escape."

"But you shouldn't forget that," said Ruby. "You came here to escape something that hurt you. You *chose* to come here. Remember the oath on your locket – watch it again."

She took her own locket from her skirt and held it up so it swung on its chain. "We've all recorded them, Cyan. We came here to get away from bad things that happened to us."

Cyan watched Ruby's locket. He eyed the sanctuary's emblem on its front – the upside-down anchor in a ring of rope – and thought back to his oath. The video he knew so well replayed itself in his head. Him sitting there, black-haired and red-eyed, hurt and begging to forget.

He shook his head, willing the image away. "But what about the good things, Ruby? It can't all have been bad. What about the *good* things we left behind?"

"Like what?"

"Like…" Cyan's mouth hung open. He closed it slowly before slumping on his bike. His eyelids were prickling again. "I… I don't remember."

Blinking the sting away, he rose again. "But that's the problem here. So much...*life* is missing. It's basically limbo. Everything's so...sometime-somewhere. I mean, how can anyone spend their life here? Can you really imagine growing old at the sanctuary, doing nothing, going nowhere?"

Ruby shrugged. "Never really thought about it."

"I didn't either. Not before I stopped taking my pills. And now that you've stopped too, I think you will as well."

Cyan hopped onto the sand and steered his quad to face north. Without a word, Ruby did the same, so that both quads were aimed at the Elsewhere Sanctuary.

After climbing back onto his quad, Cyan spoke again. "And you know what? It's not just questions that come when you're off the pills. There's more."

"Like what?"

"I didn't tell you, but when we were searching the staff floor, I started looking for the residents' files."

"You did?" Ruby's damp brow furrowed. "You said they were...next to the room with white tiles, right?"

"It wasn't just for bearings. It was because I want to remember. Before Dr Haven knocked me out he mentioned my parents. And ever since then – ever since stopping the medication – I've been getting sort of a... sense of them."

"You're remembering them?"

"No." Cyan swallowed with his throat still sore. "I don't know who they are or what they're like. Nothing like that. It's more a sense of their…absence, I guess. Of not having them. And it's getting stronger. I cried out for them this morning, when I woke up. It just flew out of my mouth. I miss them, Ruby. But I don't know them. It feels so wrong."

It was Ruby's turn to put a hand on Cyan's. He saw how sad she looked, felt a warm ache trembling in his eyelids.

His voice cracked when he went on. "It's… It's like I've realized how much I'm missing. How much I don't even know. I think that's why the bones and Ruth's note bothered me so much. All that trying to hold on; fighting not forgetting. It must have tapped into this sense of…loss I had but never recognized."

Ruby spoke softly. Her words were barely audible over the rain. "I'm so sorry, Cyan."

The pressure in Cyan's skull made him wince. He rubbed angrily at his face. "But you know what? As much as it hurts, I prefer it."

"To what?"

"To not hurting. I *want* to feel. I want…" He flinched and sucked air in through his teeth. Another swell of fiery pressure, right behind his eyes.

Ruby's hand moved up his arm. "Cyan?"

Cyan pushed a thumb and finger against his closed eyes, so that his glasses rose to his forehead. "When I get off this island," he said, "I'm going to find my parents, no matter what. I'm going to be *somewhere*. I'm so sick of being… elsewhere."

"Are you in pain?"

"It'll pass." Cyan put his hand to the ignition. "Come on. Let's get back to the sanctuary. We need to find Jonquil and the others."

Ruby shook her head, gave a slow-motion shrug. "But how, Cyan? We can't go to the staff floor again. You said so yourself: they'll be on their guard after what happened last night."

"I'm not so sure Jonquil's on the staff floor."

"Then where else could she be? We know all the other floors."

Cyan's lips curled inwards. "Something doesn't add up. There was no white-tiled room on the staff floor. And I remember now…" He closed his eyes, visualizing. "I caught a glimpse of the corridor outside that room, when Dr Haven went to fetch Mr Banter. It was all grimy and stained; nothing like the corridor on the staff floor. Plus there were no residents' files, and we checked all the rooms most likely to have them."

"What about those sheets you saw on the wall?"

Cyan shook his head. "They weren't the files. My sheet had nothing about my past or my parents. They were more like profiles. Summaries for the orderlies."

"So what are you thinking?"

"I'm thinking we need to find out – indirectly, somehow, in a low-risk way – exactly where those files are, whether they're on the staff floor or somewhere we don't know about. Wherever they are, Jonquil's a few rooms away. That's what Dr Haven said."

"And how do we find out *indirectly* –" Ruby's brow dropped cynically – "where the residents' files are?"

Cyan lifted a finger, but it faltered in the air. "I…don't know yet. That's as far as I've got. Do you have any ideas?"

A shake of the head.

"Then we'll have to figure something out. But at least we've got something to aim for. A way to narrow things down."

Ruby groaned. "Lucky us."

# TICKLESS TOCKLESS

Cyan and Ruby tore in tandem past the lighthouse with its boarded-up panes. The stone piers enveloped them both, and they roared up the ramp to a rain-drenched harbour.

The quads were soon parked. While leaving the hangar, Cyan and Ruby heard muffled bleeps.

"It's mine," said Cyan.

"Mine too."

They took out their lockets, opened them up and frowned in unison.

"Let me guess," said Cyan. "The good doctor wants you in his office?"

"Yeah. You too?"

"Yup."

Ruby's frown deepened. "You think this is something to do with our…little trip just now?"

"I hope so. I'd rather it's about that than last night."

"Oh god."

Cyan took his glasses off to dry them with his blazer. "We'd better move. It'll look fishy if we don't go right away."

When he put his glasses back on he saw that Ruby was bobbing uneasily and gnawing her lip. He touched the tips of her fingers, did his best to smile. "If this is about our trip, we've done nothing wrong. There's no rule against going far out on the sands, is there? So it'll be fine. Just act normal."

"Normal," muttered Ruby.

They headed for the sanctuary's steps.

With plimsolls squelching and blazers dripping, the pair squeezed past residents milling in the foyer. They plodded into the corridor and Cyan knocked – with what he hoped didn't sound like too much reluctance – on the director's door.

"Come in," came the voice from inside.

The lock buzzed. Cyan pushed the door. "You wanted to see us, Doctor?"

Dr Haven sat with his elbows on the desk and fingertips joined. His coat's lapels flanked a tie that was grey, immaculate, tight. He smiled genially, gesturing with long fingers at the two empty chairs facing his desk.

With the door clicking shut behind them, Cyan and Ruby took their seats.

The doctor's eyes glided – in a relaxed, unhurried way – across their faces. He said nothing.

He didn't even move. Nothing in the room did, and Cyan found himself thinking of the sandscape beyond the sanctuary – of the morning's monotony among never-ending dunes.

Something in the air turned his stomach. It was the smell of the office, perhaps; the scent of antiseptic, mingled with the damp, cloying smell that rose from his clothes.

The room was so quiet. It was hard to tell whether the doctor was even breathing.

Cyan's gaze wandered along the butterflies pinned to the walls, before lingering on the clock above the medicine cabinets; a clock with no hands, offering neither tick nor tock to break the silence.

His eyes met Ruby's for the briefest moment. She cleared her throat and smiled doggedly at the doctor. "You did want to see us, didn't you, Doctor?"

The director was in no rush to respond. He continued to gaze coolly at them both, then ended the silence with a brisk crack of his knuckles. He leaned back on his chair. "You went out on the quads today."

Ruby nodded, perhaps too keenly. "Just got back."

"You went quite far out. Further than you've ever been before."

Ruby turned to Cyan. "Is that the furthest we've been?"

Cyan frowned at one of the deep, circular windows, before giving the doctor a confused look. He spoke as innocently as he could. "How do you know how far out we went?"

"That's irrelevant," replied the doctor. "May I ask why you ventured so far?"

Ruby looked again at Cyan, who shrugged and answered. "Fancied a change?"

The director's tongue protruded slightly, before flitting across his lips. "A change…" he repeated.

"I guess," said Cyan.

"It was spur of the moment," added Ruby. "Just one of those things."

The doctor fell silent again.

Cyan's forehead felt hot beneath a fine film of sweat, but he resisted the urge to wipe it. He could see Ruby at the edge of his vision, sitting on her hands, on the brink of squirming.

"That's okay, isn't it?" asked Cyan. "Going for a long quad ride?"

Dr Haven huffed gently through his nostrils. "Of course. It's perfectly fine. There's no rule against it. It's merely a little…unusual. Our residents rarely have urges to stray so far from the sanctuary. We see to that. They also don't tend to go…fancying changes, as you put it."

The director leaned forward and returned his elbows to

the table. Cyan struggled to meet those narrowing grey eyes, so he looked down at his hands.

"So where were you going?"

Cyan's eyes shot back up to Dr Haven. "Sorry?"

"On the quad bikes today. What sort of destination did you envisage reaching?"

"Destination?"

Ruby jumped in. "No destination. We were just seeing how far we could go."

The doctor's eyes were on Ruby. "Is that so?"

"Yeah. Pushing the quads harder. Checking out their mileage."

"Mileage…" Dr Haven drew out the word, trying it on his tongue. He nodded slowly. His smile was as flat and unreadable as a blank sheet of paper.

The room fell silent. Cyan had to lower his eyes again. He gazed at the edge of the doctor's desk, wondering about its drawers – about what they might contain; whether they'd be large enough to hold the residents' files.

His eyes skimmed the office, measuring up the cabinet by the porthole window; the wide drawers at the bottom of the medicine cabinets…

But he was wasting his time. He already knew the files weren't in the doctor's office. They were next door to a white-tiled room, and the doctor's office joined only the foyer and corridor. Plus it was unlikely – impossible, even

– that Jonquil was being kept on the communal floor. And—

The director broke his train of thought: "You seem somewhat distracted, Cyan."

Cyan looked at him squarely. "I do?"

"And not in the way we try to…encourage here. You appear to be admiring my office furniture."

"I was just checking out your butterflies. I like the way you've put them all in groups." Cyan pointed a finger. "That blue one's a beauty. Any idea what it's called?"

The director's gaze didn't move to follow Cyan's finger. It remained firmly on his face.

He inhaled slowly, then cracked his knuckles again. "You can both go now. That's all."

Cyan swallowed. "That's it?"

"Why do you sound so relieved?"

Cyan laughed, and almost winced at the strain in the sound. "Just surprised, that's all." He got up with Ruby, gesturing towards the grey vinyl curtain in the corner. "Figured we were due some strobe sessions or something."

Dr Haven's eyes were still on Cyan. "No. You're not scheduled for strobe therapy today. But don't worry. You'll both be called when it's your time. We won't neglect you. We take great pains in ensuring our residents get everything they need." He picked up his pen and aimed its tip at Cyan. "You know that, don't you? You know we take care of you."

Cyan nodded vigorously. "Sure." He attempted a casual stroll to the door. Ruby tapped the button on the door frame to release its lock, and pushed hard when there was a buzz.

Cyan spun to throw a curt salute – "Sometime-somewhere, Doctor" – and they left as quickly as they could.

# TINKERING

When they entered the foyer, Cyan spotted Teal heading towards them, skirting residents with a hand in the air. "Guys! There you are! You wanna hang out now?"

As Cyan bit his bottom lip, Teal gestured towards one of the corridors. "They've got bowling in the games room today. You fancy heading over? Or are you scared of getting thrashed again?" He grinned and waggled his eyebrows.

Cyan's eyes met Ruby's. "Um. I guess...we could go?"

Teal's smile shifted into a frown. "What's up? Why are you both being so weird?"

"Weird?"

"Yeah. Like, on edge." Teal's expression darkened while he looked back and forth between them. "What are you up to? Have you still got better stuff to do? Just the two of you?"

Cyan shook his head. "It's not like that, Teal. It's—"

Ruby butted in. "We'd *love* to hang out, Teal, but I think you're wanted elsewhere."

Teal smoothed the tape on his glasses. "Oh yeah? And where's that?"

Ruby was up on her toes, searching the residents who were milling around. Cyan did the same, wondering what she was looking for.

By the far wall, beneath some vivid paintings of coral, someone tinkered on a piano that hadn't been there the day before. Cyan spotted Ms Ferryman lingering not far away, apparently enjoying the music.

Teal followed Ruby's gaze, peering around the foyer. "What's up? What're you looking for?"

"It's…Pewter," said Ruby, looking anxious now. "He was looking for you just a minute ago. Said it's really serious."

"Wh—" began Cyan, but Ruby stopped him with a discreet kick in the ankle.

"Pewter?" Teal's expression mirrored Ruby's. "Did he say why he wanted me?"

"No, but he was really worried."

The last of Teal's annoyance evaporated. He began to rub his palms together. "So where's Pewter now?"

Ruby nodded at the revolving door. "Went to check if you're on the harbour or something."

"It's pouring out there!"

Ruby nodded again, faster now. "Yeah, it's *that* serious."

Teal nibbled frantically at a fingernail. "I'd better find him."

"I'd say so. Could be bad."

"It's got to be!"

With that, Ruby spun Teal by the shoulders and shoved him towards the revolving door. "So go, Teal! Go find Pewter! Fly like the wind!"

Teal was off. The moment he was out of earshot, Cyan turned to Ruby. "What was that all about? Why'd you wind him up like that?"

"It's for a good cause. Just follow me and play along."

Together they scuttled in a speedy arc towards Ms Ferryman. Ruby called out, "Ahoy, Ms Ferryman!"

The head orderly turned her attention – somewhat irritably – from the piano to the pair of them. "Hello, Ruby. Hello, Cyan."

"You seen Teal?" Ruby pointed at the revolving door, so that Ms Ferryman looked in time to see a flustered Teal leave the building.

Ms Ferryman's neat black eyebrows lowered. "He's looking particularly tortured today."

"Yeah, Teal's been a lot worse lately. He's found something new to wind himself up about. Not that I'm sure we can do much about it."

"Can we ever?"

Ruby snorted.

"Perhaps he should visit Dr Haven," suggested Ms Ferryman.

Cyan looked cluelessly on while Ruby tutted. "That's part of the problem."

"How so?"

"It's stupid, really. Teal said that last time he was in Dr Haven's office, he saw some papers when the doctor opened a drawer."

"What's so bad about that?"

"He thinks he saw some files, and now he's got it into his head that Dr Haven isn't careful enough with keeping stuff out of sight. He's convinced there'll be some sort of slip-up, and that he'll see something about his past that messes up his treatment."

"That's highly unlikely, Ruby. You can tell Teal to stop his fussing. He'll never see anything of the sort in Dr Haven's office."

Cyan caught on to Ruby's game. He spoke to Ms Ferryman. "That's what I said. I told him residents' files'd be tucked safely away. Probably not even in Dr Haven's office."

"No, they're not."

Ruby shoved her hands into her skirt pockets. "They're probably somewhere residents can't go. Somewhere super-secure, right?"

"I assume so, since even I don't know where they are.

None of the staff are allowed to know. It's a security precaution. Only Dr Haven knows." Ms Ferryman adjusted the hem of her tunic. "But I *do* know they're kept away from this floor. Having them here would pose a risk to residents."

Cyan gave a nonchalant shrug. "Good call. Keep them safely out of reach. I'll tell Teal. Should help his latest stress-fest."

"Until he thinks of something new to agonize over."

"Too true!" hooted Ruby. She punched Cyan's arm as if he'd made the joke. "Anyway, we'd best be off. Going to the library for a bit. Sometime-somewhere, Ms Ferryman!"

"You too, Ruby. Goodbye, Cyan."

Ruby and Cyan turned to go, but faltered when Ms Ferryman called after them. "Oh, and, Cyan?"

Cyan pivoted. "Yes, Ms Ferryman?"

"How are you feeling these days?"

A sudden flush of heat beneath Cyan's collar. "How do you mean, Ms Ferryman?"

"After your fever?"

"Oh." Cyan swallowed and smiled. "Shipshape as ever, Ms Ferryman."

"So you say, but you're even paler than usual. And quiet too – by your standards, at least. You don't seem quite… yourself."

"Don't worry about me, Ms Ferryman. Nothing a

sit-down with a good book won't fix."

Ms Ferryman nodded. "Quite right. But don't hesitate to trouble Dr Haven if you're feeling out of sorts. I'm sure he'd be happy to see to you."

"I'm very sure he would. Thank you, Ms Ferryman." Cyan tapped his non-existent cap, then headed with Ruby for the corridor to the library.

Once in the corridor, Ruby murmured beneath her breath. "So only Dr Haven knows where those files are."

Cyan checked over his shoulder. They were alone. "Yeah," he whispered. "But at least we know that now." He tapped Ruby's elbow with his knuckle. "That was a sly move! You're pretty good at this stuff."

"Way better than you." Ruby gave a smug shrug. "I just saw a chance to get some clues. I know how much you love your...*intel*." She smirked at the word.

Cyan's eyes rolled behind his glasses. "Yeah, yeah, all right. But whatever you call it, it's useful information. Narrows things down. Now we can focus on Dr Haven – figure out how to get him to reveal where those files are. Then we'll have a good idea of where –" he lowered his voice further, checked the corridor again – "of where Jonquil is. And hopefully the others too."

Ruby didn't look so sure. "But Dr Haven'll be more tight-lipped about this stuff than anyone else. How can we get him to reveal where the files are?"

"We'll figure something out." Cyan led the way, and they entered the cosy hush of the library.

Cyan was brooding in a pod chair when a series of beeps sent residents reaching for lockets. Cyan pulled out his own, opened it up and saw its warning: reconfiguration in thirty minutes. He looked up at the ceiling, in the direction of the rooms that were soon to shuffle, until the locket drew back his gaze.

Cyan considered it carefully. He tilted it in his hand, so that the light from a nearby lamp flexed across its curve. Slowly, he began to nod. "Bullseye."

Ruby was on a beanbag just below him, eyeing her own locket. "Bullseye what?" she whispered.

A vague smile began to dawn on Cyan's lips. He wriggled his white eyebrows.

The longer Ruby looked at his face, the more she shook her head. "I don't like that look, Cyan. I don't like it one little bit."

TREATMENT PHASE D

# FOLLOWING DOTS

Cyan spent most of the next day in the foyer with a book, and was in the same spot the following day too, on a couch that hadn't been there the previous evening.

He held his book up to cover his face but peeked regularly over its pages to watch residents and staff leave the canteen. He and Ruby had already eaten. They'd landed the same breakfast shift, but had sat at separate tables, each of them barely touching their food.

A flash of lab coat between red uniforms: Professor Vadasz. With a coffee in one hand and a folder in the other, he left the canteen and entered the corridor that passed Dr Haven's office.

Cyan got up and made for the foyer's exit, just in time to see Professor Vadasz enter the lift at the corridor's end.

When the professor's eyes rose from the lift to the foyer, Cyan jumped into the revolving door. He walked swiftly

225

along the side of the sanctuary and pushed his book into his satchel. When he reached the corner he saw Ruby, reading on one of the benches facing the cove. She had her back to him and was thankfully alone.

"Psst."

Ruby jolted before swivelling around. "You scared me!"

"Being on standby's tense, right?"

"It's not…time, is it?"

Cyan's voice lowered. "Afraid so. The professor's heading to his office and we're both available. It's now or never."

"How about never?"

Cyan tried to look brave but it wasn't easy. He could feel his heart beating harder, spurred on by thoughts of what was coming. "You know we have to do it this way. Unless you've got any better ideas?"

Ruby put her book away and got up. "You know I haven't. Which is ridiculous, because your *plan* –" she made speech marks with her fingers – "is what you see when you look up 'stupid' in a dictionary."

Cyan bobbed tersely on the spot. They didn't have time for this. "Are you done?"

Ruby crossed her arms. "*Yes.*"

"Then let's go."

While Ruby checked around the sanctuary's corners, Cyan scanned the rear windows in case anyone was watching. The coast was clear, so they unclipped their lockets and buried them in sand by the benches.

They sped along the building's side, up its steps and into the foyer. After turning right, they paused by Ms Ferryman's door, as if waiting to go in.

When no one was looking, they ran to the restricted-access door at the corridor's end. Cyan whipped out the access card he'd stolen from the orderlies' staffroom. He swiped it through the electric lock and – with both of them flinching at its buzz – they slipped through the door and closed it behind them.

They were in the stairwell that led up to the engines and down to the staff floor. Cyan listened out; no sounds from above or below.

Ruby shook her head while whispering. "Do we really need to do this in the daytime? There'll be people about. We're *bound* to get caught."

Cyan whispered back. "After what happened on the staff floor, I think they'll be more on guard at night. They'll be less cautious during the day. Wouldn't be expecting it."

"Because it's stupidly risky."

"Yes. Because it's risky. Plus, we need Dr Haven available for this to work. You know we do." He straightened his tortoiseshell glasses. "So, let's keep going."

After they'd snuck down the stairs to the staff floor, Cyan crept to the door and peered through its window into the corridor. "We're in luck. There's a trolley not far from the professor's office. It'll—"

He ducked suddenly.

"What?" hissed Ruby.

"Technician. Just left one of the rooms."

Cyan inched his eyes back up to the pane. "It's okay. He's gone." He turned his head to Ruby, who was crouching by the door frame. "We'd better go for it. Before someone else comes. You remember what you need to do?"

A reluctant nod.

"Then here goes nothing."

Cyan pushed the door and the pair of them slinked into the corridor. They tiptoed hastily across its linoleum floor, with Ruby stopping by the professor's office to take a *DO NOT DISTURB* note from her bag and stick it to the door.

Cyan kept moving, grabbed a trolley loaded with furnishings and wheeled it back towards Ruby. When it was in position outside the professor's door, he took a folded note from his own satchel and put it on a cushion on the trolley's top.

Ruby was already crouched behind the trolley, hidden from the office doorway. Cyan lifted his fist, about to knock, when he heard a creak from down the corridor. He dropped to the floor, hid behind the trolley's narrower side and made space for Ruby.

Three orderlies left the staffroom. Their staff cards

flashed against their waists while they walked, heading to the lift at the corridor's other end. They chattered and laughed, unaware that two residents – with breath held and foreheads beading – were watching from behind a trolley.

The lift doors closed. Cyan wiped sweat from above his lip and gave Ruby a nod. He mouthed a word – "*Now*" – and shuffled back to the professor's door. Ruby returned to her position behind the trolley's wider side.

Wincing all the while, Cyan knocked on the door, then scrabbled to take cover beside Ruby. He took a white plastic cartridge from his blazer, readying its needle.

Professor Vadasz's voice came from behind the door. "Come in!"

Cyan and Ruby were silent, motionless.

"I said you can come in!"

They continued to crouch, then heard footsteps, an opening door. Through the gap beneath the trolley's upper shelf, Cyan saw trousers and the bottom of a lab coat. The coat swayed a little, and Cyan heard a papery rasp; the professor was picking up the note.

The professor read its front beneath his breath: "*For the attention of Professor Vadasz.*"

Then the crinkle of an unfolding sheet.

Cyan's palms were sticky. He clamped his lips together, doing his best to ignore the dry, flame-like crackle of the paper.

"*We're really really sorry,*" the professor read on. "*Honest.*"

Keeping close to the floor, Cyan crawled silently around the trolley's base. He steadied the cartridge in his hand and saw the lab coat swing while Professor Vadasz turned to search the corridor. "Who's sorry?" he muttered. "For wha—"

Cyan plunged the needle into the professor's thigh. Professor Vadasz gasped, stiffened and gargled, then stumbled against the door frame before sliding to the floor.

The moment he saw that the professor's eyes were shut, Cyan pocketed his cartridge, shoved the trolley back along the corridor, snatched up the note and helped Ruby drag Vadasz into the office. He shoved the professor's legs aside, so he could close and lock the door.

Ruby staggered backwards from the body. "Yuck. He's so floppy."

"Let's hope he stays that way." Cyan had already whipped the blinds down over the room's two windows. He moved to the desk and studied its computer screen. "Over here, Ruby. This is where we need you."

Ruby wiped her palms on her skirt and joined him.

"Look." Cyan's finger zipped along the dots that peppered the screen, before settling on two by the lower rear of the grid. "Those are our lockets. Keep a close eye on mine. We need to know *exactly* where it goes. When you see it back by the benches, that means I'm done. That's when you need to come join me. But be careful when you sneak off this floor."

"Really? I was planning on stamping my feet and singing at the top of my voice."

"Sarcasm's the lowest form of wit, Ruby."

"*You're* the lowest form of wit."

"You're the lowest form of anything."

Ruby walloped Cyan's arm. "You really want to do this *now*? Don't you have an idiotic plan to pull off or something?"

"I do." Cyan massaged his arm, returned to the door and gripped its handle. "Lock this door behind me. It'll buy you some time if someone ignores our do-not-disturb sign. If someone *does* try to get in, you can escape through that window. It'll take you to the side of the building."

Cyan hesitated for a moment, then let go of the handle. "In fact…" He went to the large porthole window and lifted its blind to peer through the glass. "Slight change of plan. There's no need for either of us to go back into the corridor. These windows are a safer way out."

Ruby looked at the blind and began to nod. "Good call." She raised an eyebrow. "You know, Cyan, sometimes you have your moments." Her lip began to curl. "Super-rarely, though, so don't let it go to your head."

Cyan mustered the best smile he could, but it became a twitching squint. That hot pain was back, prickling behind his eyes. It grew in fierceness while Ruby looked on.

Her forehead wrinkled. "Are you okay?"

Cyan blinked several times, trying to ease the burn. "Ruby. Listen… Whatever happens after I leave this office, I wanted to say…" His voice began to hoarsen. "I hope you'll be okay. I…I'm sorry I dragged you into this."

Ruby's eyes softened – just for a moment – before she narrowed them and jerked a thumb at the window. "You'd better get going. Otherwise this'll all be for nothing."

Cyan took in a trembling breath. "Okay. I'm going." He nodded at the computer. "Keep your eye on my locket."

# CLIPS AND CODES

Cyan released the window's latch, pushed it open and checked the sanctuary's east side. It looked safe, until a loud revving sent him ducking back into the office. He watched through the glass as some residents raced by on quads.

Once they'd disappeared into the hangar, Cyan reopened the window and dropped onto sandy flagstones. Seeing the blind fall back into place, he closed the window and sprinted to the benches behind the sanctuary. He skidded to dig up his locket, got to his feet and sprinted back the way he'd come.

The residents he'd seen on quads were leaving the hangar. Throwing a quick salute, he took the corner and vaulted up the marble steps.

A moment later he was banging on Dr Haven's door. "Hey!" he called. "I know you're in there! I heard what you said!"

A buzz from the lock. Cyan threw the door open, bolted into the office and slammed the door shut. Flushed and panting, he let his eyes dart around the room: the bench by the wall, the various cabinets, the grey vinyl curtain, the psychiatrist's couch.

His gaze fell upon the director, who was sitting at his desk, with the nib of his pen poised above an open folder.

Dr Haven gazed back. One of his grey eyebrows lifted. "Can I help you, Cyan?"

Cyan's fluster gave way to confusion. "There's… There's no one here…"

"We're here, aren't we?"

"No, I mean…" Cyan let his eyes roam the office again. "An orderly. I heard an orderly."

"We all hear orderlies." The doctor's lips creased into a smile. "They have mouths. They can speak."

"Well, yeah. But this one…" Cyan pointed back towards the door. "I was upstairs. I heard an orderly talking to someone. Said he was going to make copies of residents' files."

The director's smile faded. "That's not possible, Cyan. Orderlies don't know where those files are kept."

"This one said he'd found out – said there'd be money in using them as bribes or something. Said he was going right now to get them. But…"

Dr Haven capped his pen and placed it parallel to his

folder. "And what did this orderly look like, exactly?"

"Didn't see. I just overheard him. When I went to look there was no one there. He was gone. On the way to the files, I guess. But…" Again, Cyan scanned the room. He pushed a hand through his hair and frowned. "But there's no one here. Unless they've already stolen them? How long have you been here?"

The director didn't answer. He studied Cyan calmly. And the longer he gazed, the drier Cyan's mouth became.

It was a relief when the doctor got up. "I'm going to check on the files, as implausible as this all seems. I'm sure it's some form of misunderstanding; you must have misheard. But it's not a matter to be taken lightly." Leaving the desk, he nodded towards the bench. "Take a seat, Cyan. Don't go anywhere."

Cyan put his hands in his pockets and made sure he was in Dr Haven's path. As he stepped out of the doctor's way, he pulled out his locket and clipped it to the back of Dr Haven's coat, low enough to avoid eye level, but high enough not to dangle.

He fumbled and snapped his hand back when Dr Haven turned to look at him. "There!" blurted Cyan, with a finger flying to the window.

The director's eyes went to the glass. He gave Cyan a puzzled look. "I beg your pardon?"

"I thought… Thought I saw something."

The doctor's eyebrows met while he scrutinized Cyan's face. He nodded again at the bench. "I said sit down, Cyan."

"Oh. Yeah. Of course." Cyan shuffled backwards to take a seat.

Dr Haven left the office with the locket clipped to his coat. When the door closed, Cyan hugged himself and prayed Ruby was watching…

A little later Cyan was still in the office, doing his best to pace his breathing. His stomach and shoulders were tight with nerves.

The director finally returned.

Cyan got to his feet and – with an inquiring look on his face – walked once more into the doctor's path.

Dr Haven crossed the office, apparently lost in his thoughts. He didn't react or slow down when Cyan stooped behind him, unclipped the locket and slipped it back into his pocket.

Cyan cleared his throat. "Did you catch him?"

The director didn't respond. He stopped at his desk, took out his own staff locket, put a thumb against its screen and raised it to his mouth. "Mr Banter." He waited for a moment. "We have a potential security breach. I'd like you to change the access code to three-one-one-two. I'm not entirely sure of the exact level of threat, but until we have a more accurate assessment of the situation, I'll be changing the code every hour. Thank you."

The doctor snapped the locket shut and returned it to his pocket. He frowned abstractly at his computer until Cyan's words stirred him.

"Are the files okay, Doctor?"

Dr Haven turned his head abruptly to Cyan, as if surprised to find him in his office. He tightened his tie. "The files are fine, Cyan. We have this in hand. You can leave now."

"Good to know. Thank you, Doctor."

Cyan let himself out, cruised across the foyer and left through the revolving door. He paused on his way down the marble steps, taking deep breaths to steady his heartbeat. Gradually, his stomach began to settle.

As soon as he was ready, he strolled along the sanctuary's front, turned the corner and ran.


Scarlet – one of the sanctuary's younger residents – was sitting on a bench behind the building, staring ahead at the mossy cove.

Remembering Ruby's stunt in the foyer, Cyan approached from behind. He tapped Scarlet's shoulder. "Ahoy."

Scarlet turned to look up with her narrow brown eyes. "Ahoy, Cyan."

"I've just seen Plum on the harbour. He's looking for you. Says he's found something really cool."

Scarlet's eyes lit up. "Yeah? What is it?"

Cyan shrugged. "Dunno. Only one way to find out. Off you go." He patted her back to effectively shoo her off the bench. The second she was out of sight, he crouched and reburied his locket.

He'd only just finished when Ruby appeared. She frowned at the sand by his foot, before her eyes widened. "Oh my god. You seriously got away with it?"

Cyan nodded, then cursed when Ruby punched his arm. "You're unbelievable!" she hissed.

"What about you? Did anyone come?"

"No, but it's only a matter of time. I climbed out through the window, just like you said. Left the door locked behind me."

"So, you tracked my locket?"

Ruby bobbed on the spot with her hands clasped together. "I did!"

"Where did Dr Haven go?"

"He took the lift down. To a blank space that wasn't on the screen."

"A blank space?"

"He went *beneath* the sanctuary."

Cyan put a hand to his head. "There's another floor! That must be where he's keeping Jonquil!"

"It *has* to be." Ruby sucked in her lower lip. "I don't know how he got down there, though. He used the lift, but I saw inside the lift when we were on the staff floor. It only had buttons for floors one, two and three."

"That's the staff, communal and engine floors."

"Exactly. No button for an underground floor."

Cyan frowned at his feet, then looked up and clicked his fingers. "He uses a code. Three-one-one-two. That's what gets the lift to take you down."

Ruby turned her head a little but kept her eyes on Cyan. "How'd you know the code?"

"I heard it in Dr Haven's office. He told Mr Banter to change it. Three-one-one-two."

"He let you hear that?"

Cyan froze, struck by a thought. "Hang on. He said he'd change the code every hour." He gripped Ruby's elbow. "If we want to use that lift, we need to do it now."

"Now? *Right* now? But…" Her chest rose and fell. "Shouldn't we get a plan together first?"

"No time! This is our only chance, Ruby! If we don't go now the code'll change, and then we'll never get to that hidden floor!"

Ruby's shoulders sank. "But we can't. It's too…too…"

"Come on!" Cyan tugged her hand and began to move, but she pulled her fingers away.

Cyan looked at her desperately, his eyes pleading.

"Please, Ruby. We *have* to use this opportunity. For Jonquil's sake. And all the others!"

"Wait a minute. Just wait." Ruby swallowed deeply and closed her eyes.

When they reopened she was glaring at Cyan. "Okay," she said. "I'm coming. But if this goes wrong, I promise you Dr Haven will be the *least* of your worries."

Cyan took her hand again, slowly this time, holding it between his palms. "Thanks, Ruby. I—"

She shoved his hand away. "Just go."

# DEEPER STILL

They were soon standing by the door to Dr Haven's office. Ruby pretended she was poised to knock, while Cyan peered down the corridor to watch the foyer. No one was looking, so he dashed to the lift and swiped his stolen access card. The doors parted and Cyan darted in.

As soon as Ruby was with him, he punched the lift's buttons: three-one-one-two. The doors closed and the lift began its descent.

The number two button blinked off.

The number one button blinked on.

The number one button blinked off, and still the lift descended.

Ruby moved to the lift's front corner, doing her best to hide behind the doorway's edge. Cyan went to the opposite corner, doing the same.

There was a gentle bump.

The doors opened.

Cyan listened for sounds from beyond the lift. He heard only a faint, rhythmic whirring, accompanied by thin, regular chirps.

Holding his breath, he peered cautiously around the doorway's edge. The lift had opened onto a long corridor like the one on the staff floor, but with a linoleum floor that was scuffed and stained. Its concrete walls were cold and bare, without plaster or paint. Bulbs in cage-like fittings hung from the ceiling, spilling out a low light that dimmed and flickered.

Cyan heard the nerves in Ruby's whisper. "What on earth's that noise?"

He cocked his ear. That ominous whirring still filled the dim corridor. And those shrill electronic chirps – like the trills of mechanical birds, scared and trapped in cages…

He whispered back. "No idea. But it looks like no one's around. Better send the lift back to the foyer, before someone notices it's down here."

Ruby nodded gravely and pressed the number two button. They stepped out with the doors closing behind them.

"I don't like this," whispered Ruby.

"Me neither." Cyan eyed a red-brown stain on the rubbery floor by his feet. "Let's get searching. If we hang about talking, we're going to get caught."

The whirring grew louder as they crept along the corridor. Cyan tried the first door on the right, but found only chipped shower cubicles, dirty floor tiles, rusty metal hoses.

Hearing Ruby whisper his name, he followed her to a corridor that branched off to the left. It was straight and long, with doors lined up along both walls.

He gestured at the small, luminous rectangles attached at head-height to each door. "What are those things?"

"Screens, I think."

They tiptoed to the first door on the right. Their mouths fell open when they saw its screen.

"Oh god," breathed Ruby.

Filmed from somewhere above, a boy no older than twelve trudged slowly up and down a small, grimy room. The cramped space had padded walls and a scuffed rubber floor, and was empty apart from a thin metal bed and low steel toilet.

Cyan peered closer at the screen. The boy was barefoot and wore a grey hospital gown. His arms were tightly crossed while he paced, with his fingers digging deep into raw, bruised skin.

Ruby shuddered. "He must be in there. Behind that door."

Cyan tried the handle but it wouldn't move. He found his staff card and whipped it through the slot by the door,

243

only to get a buzz and a red light. Still the handle refused to budge.

Ruby was venturing further into the corridor. Her gaping eyes caught the glow from its screens. "There're loads of them," she croaked. "Loads…"

Cyan tried the handles of the next few doors. Each screen showed identical padded rooms with identical beds and toilets. And every room held a solitary resident.

He hugged himself as if the temperature had dropped. "This is them," he whispered. "Dr Haven's…casualties."

Some lay on their beds, curled into shivering, bony balls. Some paced, shook and shouted without making a sound; the rooms must have been soundproofed. Others sat on the floor, hunched against walls with their faces ground into their knees. At least three of them had raw, red bald patches where hair had once been, and Cyan spotted bandaging behind ears and above necks.

One resident looked vaguely familiar; a pale teen with a bob of ragged blonde hair. After squinting for some moments, Cyan realized where he'd seen her before: on a photo in the orderlies' staffroom.

"Amber?" He swiped his card through the door's slot. But again, the buzz and red light.

Frustrated, he moved along the next two doors. When he saw the second door's screen he gasped and shook his head, struggling to believe his eyes. "Jonquil…"

He almost didn't recognize her. Her black hair was lank and tangled, and she looked thinner, with her neck and cheeks gaunt and sallow. She was lying rigidly on her metal bed. Her bare arms trembled on its rubbery mattress.

Cyan tried his card, this time more slowly, but yet again: the buzz and red light.

He grunted in anger. "The card's not working. There must be limited staff access. We need to find a card that works. Maybe there's one on this floor." His eyes searched the corridor. "There's got to be. We should split up and look."

He backtracked the way he'd come. "We'll do the same as before. I'll try the rooms on the left; you do the ones on the right. Okay?"

With eyes agape and her mouth wide open, Ruby stared back and forth between Cyan and the screens. "I… I just can't believe this. I mean…I know what you told me. But I can't believe they'd… Not like this…"

"*Card*," hissed Cyan. "We need to find a card that opens these doors. You take the rooms on the right, okay?"

Ruby's head twitched in what Cyan took to be a yes. Nodding in reply, he checked around the corner, then skulked back into the main corridor. As he brushed past a metal trolley, that whirring hum – more sinister than soothing – filled the chill air. The bulbs above him blinked and stuttered.

The next room on the left was more than halfway along the corridor. The light beneath its door was lambent white, and that drone-like whirring came from within. Cyan opened the door a crack to peer inside. He saw polished linoleum flooring, pale grey walls, snatches of white metal and plastic.

No one seemed to be about, so he let himself in.

The whirring came from a machine that filled half the room. It looked like a swollen, white plastic tunnel, long enough to fit the bed attached by rails to its shadowy mouth. There was another plastic bed not far from the first, with what Cyan recognized as X-ray machinery suspended above. Thick cables slinked from both machines to a white booth, with computer screens visible behind its darkened glass.

Seeing no sign of access cards, Cyan neared the dark doorway at the room's far end. Leaving white light behind, he stepped carefully into a much smaller space. His eyes slid from left to right, adjusting to the dim, greenish glow.

Every inch of every wall was covered in sheets of dark plastic, arranged as neatly as the butterflies in Dr Haven's office. Images of grey, blue and green glowed against black gloss. Cyan realized he was looking at scans and X-rays, stuck to illuminated walls.

Cranial cross-sections were arranged in meticulous rows, as if a brain had been thinly sliced and pinned up for scrutiny. Some cross-sections went from the side of the head rather than the top, so that Cyan could see noses and throats, grooves of grey matter. Glowing skulls grinned at him from every direction, while others looked sidelong to reveal grey vertebrae, hanging down like chains of bone.

A spurt of nausea hit Cyan's stomach. After glancing around for access cards, he reversed out of the gloom and nearly tripped over a cable while stumbling backwards through the larger room.

With his face set and pale, Cyan continued along the corridor, and slipped through its final door to find a room he remembered all too well.

White tiles and halogen lights. A row of trolley beds. A metal cabinet and stainless-steel sink. This was where he'd been injected with water and sedated, before waking up days later in the medical quarters upstairs.

Still no hint of cards, so Cyan moved quickly to the door at the room's other end. This time it wasn't locked. Peeping carefully around its edge, Cyan found a narrow space filled with filing cabinets.

He stepped inside and opened the nearest cabinet. There were no access cards, but after opening another drawer he realized he'd found something else.

The residents' files.

Cyan had to move on – to keep looking for access cards. But he couldn't help lingering.

He reached out, about to flick through the files. Then he froze, scolding himself, and slid the drawers shut. There was no time.

It took some effort to back away. Cyan tried the door opposite the one he'd come through. It opened and – peering through the crack – he saw that the next room was also deserted.

Cyan stepped inside. His nostrils flared and his stomach fluttered. The air was caustic with antiseptic.

This room was as harshly lit as the last. The breath caught in Cyan's throat. He'd stumbled upon an operating theatre.

Surgical lights loomed like huge insect eyes over an operating table. And by the table's side: a small trolley topped with stainless steel instruments.

Cyan shivered at the sight of scalpels, scissors, clamps and saws – even a surgical hammer and drill – all lined up in perfect parallel. Box-like machines surrounded the operating table, each of them covered in screens and dials, wires and tubes.

Cyan stood transfixed, until sudden sounds made him hunch on the spot.

Footsteps, echoing in the corridor. The clop of hard soles, leisurely but firm – certainly not Ruby's.

And they were getting closer.

# BAIT

Cyan whirled to face the door. He tilted an ear, trying to pinpoint where the footsteps were coming from. They dulled and lost their echo, but sounded closer now, perhaps next door.

Cyan crouched behind the operating table. He held his breath, listening out.

The footsteps faded, then echoed again through the corridor. And then, the click of an opening door. A frightened cry. Ruby.

Cyan shot up from cover, heard scuffing shoes and smothered shrieks. A loud slam followed by frantic banging – the sound of fists against a metal door.

Cyan was already on the move. He launched himself towards the corridor but stumbled to a stop before leaving the theatre. He saw Dr Haven ahead, passing through the white-tiled room, strolling towards him.

The director stepped through the filing room and smiled warmly from the operating theatre's doorway. "Hello, Cyan. Or as you residents like to say, ahoy." He lifted a finger to his head – a parody tap of an imaginary cap.

Cyan glared. "Where's Ruby?"

"Safely out of the way."

The doctor turned towards the thumping sound from the corridor, calling out. "You can stop guarding the lift, Mr Banter! I've located both of them. Cyan's in the operating theatre. Didn't I say he'd be near the files?"

"You…" Cyan's tongue moved drily in his mouth. "You knew we'd be here?"

The doctor regarded him with some amusement. "Of course I knew. I helped you to get down here. You don't honestly think I'd divulge a passcode with a resident in my office, do you?"

Confusion twisted Cyan's features. "But how? How did you know I was trying –" his startled eyes roved the theatre – "trying to find this place?"

"Well. It was quite clear that someone was up to no good. First a mysterious intrusion on the staff floor; toppled glasses and a missing access card. And then your little excursion, far out on the sands. Residents don't usually – how did you put it? – *fancy a change*. I ensure our medication curbs any urge to…rock the boat, if you'll pardon the expression."

One side of Dr Haven's mouth curled upwards. "And then, not long after that, you come running into my office, with an absurd tale about an orderly stealing residents' files. I noticed, of course, that you'd done something to the back of my coat. If I were you, Cyan, I'd steer well clear of a career in pickpocketing.

"As soon as I was in the corridor, I had a look and there it was: your locket, clipped to my coat. It doesn't take a genius to see what you were attempting to do. I wasn't at all surprised to receive a call from the staff floor, shortly after I'd dismissed you from my office; Professor Vadasz had been found unconscious in his room. Which confirmed my suspicion: I was being tracked."

The doctor let out a sigh. "Before that, when I'd just found your locket on my coat..." His thin tongue darted across his lips. "I decided to play along with your game. I gave you everything you needed: the location of the residents' files and the code for the lift. I didn't really call Mr Banter while you were in my office; I merely announced the code, and invented a fiction about an hourly code change, to ensure you'd be down here soon. And here you are." He pinched his long fingers together, before moving them sideways across the air. "Checkmate."

Cyan's breaths came short and sharp. He felt hot and faint and struggled to pull the sterile air into his lungs. "But why'd you... Why did you guide us here?"

Dr Haven drummed his fingertips together. "When you suspect that some of your lab rats are misbehaving, Cyan, the best way to identify them is to leave them to it, until they inevitably give themselves away. And when they've done so, you offer what they want as bait, and you lure them into a trap.

"I knew you couldn't be working alone; not if someone was tracking your locket. And of course, it was Ruby. She's the one who joined you far out on the sands. It's her locket that's presently with yours behind the institute.

"And now I have both of you exactly where I want. Two naughty little rats, trapped and tucked away down here, where no one will ever intrude. And I can do whatever I want with you. Anything at all."

The doctor entwined his fingers. Cyan recoiled at the crack of bony knuckles.

"Naughty rats," continued Dr Haven, "need to be taught a lesson. They need to be dealt with so that they're never naughty again. The last thing we want is for their naughtiness to upset the other rats or – even worse – give them ideas. It's…"

He trailed off when Mr Banter entered the theatre. The huge orderly made the doctor look gaunt, sharp, funereal.

"Thank you for joining us, Mr Banter." Dr Haven turned his ear once more to the corridor; the thumping had stopped. "It sounds like Ruby's settled down. We can

**252**

deal with her shortly, but first I have some business here to attend to."

He put a thin, immaculate finger to his chin, scrutinizing Cyan. "I'm very curious, you see, about the cause behind the effect. What exactly sent you and Ruby down here, Cyan? Did you go to all of this trouble simply to look at your files?"

Cyan replied through gritted teeth. "*Jonquil.*" His hands curled into balls. "It was Jonquil. That's what brought us down here."

One of Dr Haven's eyebrows rose, before sinking to meet the other. "Is that so? And what do you know of…Jonquil?"

"I know everything. I know your treatment damaged her. I know you hid her away, wiped her from everyone's memory."

The director's smile tightened. He lowered his head, considering Cyan closely. "And how could you possibly know about Jonquil? You were treated along with all the other residents."

"No." Cyan allowed himself a grim smirk. "I swapped the filth in your syringe with water. And then *I* played along."

"But…" Dr Haven's eyelids fluttered. His mouth opened – just enough to bare a sliver of teeth – and he nodded slowly. "Ah. Of course. You must have swapped the drug while I fetched Mr Banter. And the water…" A flash of those grey, glassy eyes. "That explains your fever after the treatment. The bacteria in tap water is fine in the digestive system, but not so much in the bloodstream."

He considered this, then began nodding in approval. "That was actually quite clever of you, Cyan. Admirable initiative. But I'm afraid your more recent strategy – the indiscreet prying, your implausible bluffs and clumsy locket work… That wasn't clever at all. It was downright inept. I'm a little disappointed, if I'm honest. I'd never have expected such poor attempts at subterfuge from someone of your intelligence. Then again, it does fit your personality profile. The recklessness of it. The…*audacity*."

The doctor's face darkened. He inhaled sharply through his nostrils, and that affable smile returned. "Well, Cyan. If you faked your amnesia, you'll no doubt remember our little exchange in the room behind me. You'll know what went wrong with Jonquil; how the Lethe Method caused irreversible damage to the poor thing."

"Yes!" spat Cyan. He flung an arm towards the wall on the right. "I know about the others too, all damaged like Jonquil and hidden in cells! And I bet they won't be the last!"

The director's lips drooped. A mockery of regret. "I daresay they won't. Unfortunately, the method has some considerable way to go. But you know what they say: if at first you don't succeed…"

He laughed then, with mild-mannered pleasure. "You

and Ruby will soon have first-hand experience of what those residents went through. The repression that does so much damage to you all, all that hidden conflict… I don't yet know how to prevent it, but I certainly know how to *accelerate* it. I'll do so for you and Ruby, down here, in my own time. And I'll enjoy doing so, thoroughly. It's nice, don't you think, when business is also pleasure?"

While the director beamed, Cyan fought the trembling in his limbs. He jabbed his finger at the ceiling. "But everyone else!" He tried to sound strong, but his words came out guttural and cracked. "Up there… If we're missing they'll—"

"They'll what?" interrupted Dr Haven. He chuckled. "You know very well what will happen up there, Cyan. A few strobe sessions are all it takes. First you and Ruby will become…hazy in residents' minds. They'll be confused, for a spell, but they'll take their medicine and they won't think twice about it. And before you know it – *pop* – no one remembers you at all. You and Ruby will be practically dead to them. Worse than dead, in fact. You'll never have existed in the first place."

With his eyes scouring the floor, Cyan tried to find words. When he looked up, a shiver coursed from his spine to the back of his legs. He'd never seen Dr Haven grin. It was all teeth and thin skin, and brought to mind the skulls he'd fled from next door.

Cyan's throat began to swell. "But how...*how* can you do this? You and the staff..." His pupils flickered to Mr Banter. "How can you all do this? And...and to *children*?"

"Poor boy," crooned Dr Haven. He turned briefly to Mr Banter and they exchanged droll looks. "You're even less informed than you think. Only Mr Banter and I know about this floor. As far as the staff are aware, the residents who have breakdowns are sent to a separate rehabilitation centre, where they make speedy recoveries and live the happiest, most contented of lives. The staff don't ask questions. They're paid well not to."

The director shrugged. "You think we avoid CCTV here just to keep you residents at ease? It's better if staff don't know about my extracurricular activities. They might not approve of the treatment's more...experimental elements. Sadly, some people are prone to ethical pretentions. Not everyone's as committed to science and the greater good as Mr Banter and myself."

Cyan tensed as hard as he could, doing his best to stop his shaking. He felt anger boiling in the pit of his stomach, burning away his fear. "Don't talk about science and the greater good! I remember what you said before. This is about making money."

The director breathed onto one of his cufflinks. He polished it while speaking. "The money's merely a bonus. As I said, Cyan: it's nice when business is pleasure."

"You won't get away with this." Cyan's voice was rising. He found himself straightening up, with fists clenched and knuckles whitening. "All these people disappearing... People will ask questions! They'll come looking! There'll be parents, authorities..."

A tut from Dr Haven. "I assure you, there won't. We're very careful in our recruitment of residents. We take in juvenile strays and runaways. Lost causes. Children with young, limited memories and nothing to lose. No one ever comes looking for them. And even if they did, the people who invest in this sanctuary are wealthy and powerful. They ensure our island remains a blind spot and cover our tracks wherever necessary. This sanctuary attracts support from very influential people, Cyan; people willing to sacrifice for a nobler cause."

Cyan sneered. "But they're not sacrificing themselves, are they. They're sacrificing others. They're sacrificing people who are suffering and vulnerable."

A resigned shrug from the director. "The way of the world, I'm afraid. Now, Cyan, I have a little something for you." He turned to Mr Banter. "Keep an eye on him, will you? I won't be a moment."

# A PARTING GIFT

The doctor disappeared through the doorway, leaving Cyan alone with Mr Banter.

While Cyan pursed his lips and took deep, angry breaths, the orderly smiled contentedly, with eyes bright and blue behind his glasses.

Dr Haven soon returned and tossed a folder across the room. It skidded across the floor, before coming to a stop by Cyan's feet.

"What's this?" asked Cyan.

"Your resident's file. Everything's in there. Your real name. Where you came from. Why you came here."

Cyan stared at the file. Then he crouched to reach out with a slow, trembling hand. But he hesitated, just before touching the folder.

He lifted his gaze to Dr Haven, who was watching him with some curiosity. "Why are you giving me this?"

"No reason."

Cyan's eyes narrowed. "Is this for your research? Will you be making notes?" He looked at the wall to his right. "Or is this how it begins – how you start making me like the residents in those cells?"

Dr Haven brushed some lint from his waistcoat. "A little of both. Perhaps something more. Think of this as a parting gift, before we lose you for good. For all of your cockiness, Cyan, I was fond of you, in some ways. You were always one of our more interesting specimens."

Cyan stood up and rolled back his shoulders. The folder lay untouched on the floor. "I'm not a *specimen*, and I don't want that file. I'm not going to give you the satisfaction."

"Come now, Cyan. You must be ever so intrigued."

Cyan tried to keep his eyes on the director, but it was impossible. He couldn't stop his head from lowering. His gaze fell to the file by his feet.

"I can see you're tempted," said Dr Haven. "Perhaps some snippets will motivate you. How about if I say… Nicholas Bromden? That's your name, Cyan. Your *real* name. And what if I also say…Joni? Or Scott? Scott and Joni Bromden, your—"

"Parents," said Cyan. He was still looking at the folder. His shoulders began to sink. All the fight in his stance was gone.

"That's right. Would you like to know more? It's all there for you, in that file."

Morosely, but with eyes still glued to the folder, Cyan shook his head.

"How about," continued Dr Haven, "if I mention fire? A fire in the family home. Hm?"

Cyan couldn't even shake his head. He stood there, immobile, with his neck crooked. His windpipe became tight and ticklish. He could almost smell the smoke, coarse and thick in his nostrils and throat. He put a hand to his face, felt the heat coursing across his cheek.

"I think," said Dr Haven, "you have an inkling of where this story's going."

Cyan pushed his hands against his ears. He could hear the distant crackling of wood. Closing his eyes, he saw blistering paint, billowing smoke – walls and curtains eaten by flame. Someone was wailing through the roar, crying through the heat – strangled and sorrowful sounds, at once familiar and unknown.

The doctor raised his voice so Cyan could hear him. "The curious thing, though, is that it wasn't the fire that killed your mother. Not as such. She stayed with your father in the building, trying to find you. You were too frightened to escape, lost in all the smoke. Just a twelve-year-old boy. The three of you got out alive. It seemed all would be well."

Something acrid was pooling beneath Cyan's tongue. His eyelids began to sting and he clamped them shut, trying to stave off the pressure that was building behind his eyes. His shaking hands fell from his ears.

The doctor went on. "But your mother died in hospital, sadly. There were complications, from all the smoke she'd inhaled.

"I remember you saying, when you first arrived here – before you filmed your oath – that it wasn't just her passing that upset you. It was the fact that she'd survived the fire only to die anyway. How cruel to be given hope, only to have it torn away.

"That's what really tortured you, Cyan. That and the guilt, of course. I daresay your mother would have lived, if she hadn't stayed in the house to save you."

A pained whimper left Cyan's lips.

Dr Haven tutted. "It's hardly surprising that your father turned to alcohol. You told me you were frightened by how quickly you became invisible to him. All he did was drink; he was completely lost without your mother. Lost, and pretty much…dead too. That's how you phrased it, Cyan. And though your father never said as much, you felt he blamed you for your mother's death. You blamed yourself, after all.

"It's no wonder you left home and ran away." The director gave a wistful sigh. "It's all so terribly tragic, isn't it? I had no doubt you'd accept a place here at the sanctuary. You were a perfect candidate."

Cyan was barely aware of the fact that he'd sunk to his knees. The pain behind his eyes was liquid fire. He threw down his glasses and pushed his palms against his eyelids.

"They loved you so very much, Cyan. You said so yourself. And you can see it in every visual record in that file. We have all the photos that survived the fire. We gathered every picture available to us online and off. Beaches and tents. School nativity plays. Blowing out candles on birthday cakes. Your mother was pretty. And you had your father's dark hair – until it all turned white."

Try as he might, Cyan still couldn't remember his parents' faces. All that came back to him was the fear and the smoke, the grief and the flames.

And the love. The fierce love that kindled the hurt and fanned the sorrow.

Cyan pulled his hands from his eyes. He looked at Dr Haven, who'd stepped forward to watch him more closely.

"It hurts, doesn't it?" said the doctor. He was flexing his lips downwards, trying to look sad. But even without glasses, Cyan saw glee in his eyes. The pain writhed and wrenched in his gut, twisting into bitterness and gall.

"Sometimes it's best to forget," soothed Dr Haven. "Don't you think so? Can you see now what I'm offering to the world, Cyan, if I manage to get this treatment right?"

Cyan's jaw ached. He'd been grinding his teeth.

Scowling, he took his glasses from the floor, put them on and looked the director straight in the eye. "I don't *want* to forget. I don't want to lose the pain. Never again. It's part of me. It's how my *mum's* still part of me. My dad too. I'd rather…*hurt* than forget!"

He lifted his glasses to swipe a hand across his eyes and was surprised to feel something damp. When he realized what it was, he gasped and stared at his knuckles.

And there it was: a tear streak, glimmering in the harsh white light.

He looked up. Dr Haven was staring too.

The director scratched the side of his bald patch. "How curious. It appears someone's been skipping their medicine. That certainly explains a thing or two."

His eyes shifted to Cyan's face. That ghoulish grin returned. "Say what you want, Cyan, but I'm afraid you *will* forget. I'll see to it personally that you do."

He looked again at the streak on Cyan's hand. "I'll allow you that tear. But everything else will stay locked up, so that it can rot you away from the inside. Just like it's rotting every resident in those cells."

He stepped aside. "Now if you'd be so kind, Mr Banter, put him to sleep."

Mr Banter, with a pearly smile spreading across his face, approached Cyan. He took a pale cartridge from his starched, white trousers.

Cyan stooped to clutch the file in his hand. With his eyes never leaving the orderly, he shifted into a crouch and held up the folder, so that it hid the cartridge he'd eased from his blazer.

"It's too late to look at that file," said Dr Haven. "You had your chance."

Mr Banter was almost upon him. Those teeth – as pristine and white as his uniform – looked tiny and copious, as if there were too many for his mouth. He twirled the cartridge in his thick pink fingers. A long needle glittered at its end.

While still holding the file in one hand, Cyan tightened his grip on the cartridge in the other. His expression twitched beneath a film of sweat, flitting between terror and resolve. He could hear the orderly's breathing, steady and loud, forced from huge, bellow-like lungs.

Mr Banter poised his needle, bracing to strike. But his smirk vanished when the cartridge flew from his hand, knocked aside by Cyan's folder.

Throwing the file into Mr Banter's face, Cyan sidestepped and plunged his own needle into the orderly's thigh. Mr Banter winced and gaped in bewilderment at the cartridge jutting from his leg.

Cyan snatched the hammer from the trolley and dashed at Dr Haven, who was blocking his way out. Trembling and panting, Cyan drew the hammer back, threatening to strike.

The doctor's eyes were on the hammer's silver head. "You wouldn't hurt me." His gaze moved to Cyan's face. "It goes against your profile."

He reached out to take the hammer, but Cyan took a swing that forced him to whip back his hand.

Cyan raised the hammer again. "You really want to test my profile today, *Doctor*?"

Scowling, the doctor backed away.

After throwing a glance at Mr Banter – who was staring at his leg and waiting for the drug to kick in – Cyan ran past filing cabinets and through the white-tiled room.

The moment he hit the corridor, he heard Dr Haven shouting at Mr Banter. "It's *empty*, you oaf! He used it on the professor! Pick up your own and get that boy!"

"Ruby!" cried Cyan, desperate to find her. He was sprinting for the lift when he spotted a chair wedged against a door just ahead. He kicked it aside and pulled the door open to see Ruby getting up. She was in a room full of storage boxes, leather-strapped beds and more chairs.

"Cyan!" She ran to the doorway. "Dr Haven! He found me and jammed the—"

"No time!" Cyan pulled her into the corridor.

265

Dr Haven was strolling towards them, with Mr Banter lumbering by his side. While the doctor's expression was calm and unruffled, Mr Banter glared through his glasses at Cyan. Those thick lenses only magnified his fury. His fists bulged and clenched at the ends of his trunk-like arms.

"Come on!" Cyan yanked Ruby's arm, but she didn't move.

"*Wait.*" Ruby was looking at Mr Banter, her pupils searching his muscly bulk. She slipped her hand from Cyan's, pressed a palm to his chest, then began walking away, towards the director and orderly.

"What are you doing?" shouted Cyan. He stepped forward with an arm outstretched, but Ruby was beyond reach.

She didn't even look back. "There's no getting away," she said. "We're better off handing ourselves in."

Cyan watched helplessly, his face crumpling in despair.

Ruby gave Mr Banter her arm. Dr Haven looked smugly on. "At least Ruby sees sense, Cyan. Your pointless gallivanting merely delays the inevitable. It's a waste of—"

"*Go!*" It was Ruby. She'd yanked the card from the clip on Mr Banter's waist and, with a flick of her elbow, sent it spinning through the air. "Get it, Cyan!"

Cyan didn't need to be told. He bolted along the corridor, slid on his knees and plucked the card from the floor. While twirling to sprint back the way he'd come, he glimpsed Mr Banter ramming his needle into Ruby's neck.

Cyan continued to run. He could hear Mr Banter catching up behind him, pummelling the floor with his heavy feet.

In a half-skid, half-stumble, Cyan launched the trolley he'd passed earlier and sent it speeding towards Mr Banter. It slammed the orderly's legs and sent him into a stagger, before being smashed sideways into the wall. Squeals of twisted metal filled the corridor.

The trolley had bought Cyan a few seconds. Still gripping Mr Banter's access card, he faltered by the corridor lined with residents' cells. But Mr Banter was charging at him again and – seeing that the corridor led to a dead end – Cyan made for the lift, jumped in and slammed the button.

Mr Banter was almost upon him. The lift's doors were closing, but they wouldn't shut in time. Panicking, Cyan lobbed his hammer into the corridor. Mr Banter threw himself aside, barely dodging the whirring steel.

The doors continued to close and – through the narrowing gap – Cyan saw Ruby unconscious at Dr Haven's feet, and Mr Banter snarling and charging, storming bull-like towards him.

Mr Banter's face, still closing in, writhed red with rage. But the lift's doors met and – though they rang with pounding fists – the face was gone.

# NO-ZONE

While the lift ascended, Cyan pushed Mr Banter's card deep into his pocket. He leaned with his forearms against the metal wall, taking huge breaths to steady his trembling.

When the doors parted, Cyan sped past Dr Haven's office and burst into the foyer. The space was bustling with residents in red, and Cyan saw two orderlies chatting to one side of the handless clock. Their conversation stopped abruptly as they pulled their lockets from their trousers.

Cyan waved his arms at them. "Don't do it!" he yelled. "Whatever Dr Haven says, don't do it!" He pointed frantically at the corridor behind him. "There's an extra floor! He's keeping residents locked up – the ones you thought were sent away! He's using us for experiments!" He gestured feverishly at the residents who'd stopped to stare.

The orderlies exchanged baffled glances, then opened their lockets to check the messages on their screens. When they looked again at Cyan their gazes had hardened. A sudden resolve seemed to tighten their shoulders.

More orderlies were marching into the foyer. Cyan saw the glint of open lockets in their hands. Their expressions were steely and serious, with eyes that scanned the residents before settling on Cyan.

Ms Ferryman – with her own locket in hand – entered from the corridor to her office. She saw Cyan. A look of worry wrinkled her brow.

Cyan stepped back with his palms rising. "Please!" he cried. "If Dr Haven's telling you to grab me, don't listen! He's experimenting on us all – hiding sick residents! Everyone's in danger! Please believe—"

"*Nonsense.*"

All eyes looked past Cyan, and he turned to see Dr Haven at the foyer's edge. Mr Banter was beside him. The orderly looked less rattled now – placid and professional.

"Orderlies." The director spoke loudly, but with a tone as serene as his smile. "Be so kind as to ignore Cyan's ravings. The poor boy's having an episode of mania. He's showing severe symptoms of delusion. Keep your distance and block the exits. Mr Banter will sedate and remove him."

Several residents were in Mr Banter's way. They shuffled awkwardly on their feet. Some stepped timidly aside, with their gazes shifting back and forth between Cyan and the director.

"I'm telling the truth!" wailed Cyan. He looked with pleading eyes at Ms Ferryman, then turned to the residents closest to him, a couple of whom had backed away. "They'll knock you out and make you forget!" His voice broke. He could feel the spit spraying from his lips. "Don't let it happen! Fight them!"

Some of the orderlies exchanged glances. Residents looked at each other; a collective murmur began to rise.

Dr Haven had to shout over the voices. "Everyone move out of Mr Banter's way! Cyan is dangerous and liable to hurt someone!" The doctor's eyes scoured the foyer. Some jittery residents were trying to flee the scene, pressing against the orderlies blocking all exits. But a faltering crowd was still in Mr Banter's path.

"Fine!" barked the director. He shook his fist in the air. "Orderlies: standard protocol! Round them up – *all* residents – and put them to sleep! Mr Banter: *take Cyan!*"

Mr Banter shoved residents aside and began to move. He was drawing closer to Cyan, with Dr Haven walking just behind.

Cyan twisted to and fro. He saw an orderly by the revolving door. Others were guarding the staircases and corridors. There was only one way to go: deeper into the throng.

He pushed his way through the crowd, which became increasingly unsettled when Mr Banter started tossing children aside like dolls. When the orderlies took out their needles, the tumult only got worse.

Cursing and barging, and with Mr Banter closing relentlessly in, Cyan kept searching for a way out. Something caught his eye: an orderly had left his post to grapple with a resident; the stairs to the upper rooms were clear.

While Cyan bounded up the spiralling steps, a cold laugh followed from below. "You've trapped yourself!" yelled Dr Haven. "I'll order a reconfiguration and fill the framework with staff! There's nowhere to go! Stop this foolishness!"

Cyan kept climbing. He heaved at the bannister and – after losing his footing – scrabbled the rest of the way on all fours.

When he hit the upper rooms, he heard beeps from lockets. The shuffle was coming.

He bolted through a door into a hallway and saw two bewildered residents climbing into snugs. Deep sounds reverberated through the floor and walls. Distant squeals. The grind of cogs and pulleys.

Cyan jumped instinctively towards an empty snug but skidded when its rear opened up. A technician climbed out and dropped into the wooden hollow. He grimaced at Cyan, with his arms rising to grab him.

As Cyan backed away he heard something else over the hum of the walls: pounding footsteps. He glanced backwards and saw Mr Banter through the door's window, charging towards him with his fists clenched.

Cyan ran. He barrelled from one room to the next, darting in random directions and praying Mr Banter wouldn't brave the shuffle. But even when the walls began to move, Mr Banter kept coming.

The floor beneath Cyan's feet slid to the right, while the door ahead coasted left. He veered in a sharp diagonal line; Mr Banter's hands just missed him as he leaped through the gliding door into a bedroom.

Mr Banter was quick for someone his size. Whenever Cyan hurled himself through a gap between shifting walls, the orderly made it through too, just a hair's breadth behind.

Cyan caught glimpses of red, white and grey; residents and staff, gawping from their snugs. He headed up a spiral staircase, felt his stomach hit his lungs when the room lurched downwards.

An unfamiliar voice, gruff and deep, came from below. "I'm going to enjoy this, Cyan!"

Cyan glanced down. He saw Mr Banter grinning around the corner of the stairway, and almost stumbled with the shock. "You can talk!"

Mr Banter guffawed, his laughter huge and thick against

the squeal and din. "I can do more than that! You'll find out soon enough – when I get my hands on your tiny little neck!"

Cyan gritted his teeth. His legs were tired and aching; his throat was gasping and raw. Topping the staircase, he threw himself at an opening to the left, but a rising wall caught his chin and knocked him back towards the stairs.

A chink in his vision; his glasses were cracked.

Mr Banter appeared and lunged for him, but Cyan managed to stagger and dodge. He shouldered a door that rose into view, then jumped through it onto a floor that was lowering away.

Cyan vaulted an unmade bed. Something smashed above him and a downpour of shards hit his head. He saw broken chunks of vase by his feet, then peered backwards to see another vase in Mr Banter's hand, raised and ready for throwing.

He dodged to the right as it shattered to his left, but his manoeuvre sent him bouncing off shelves and knocking over plants.

Looking backwards again, Cyan glimpsed a plant pot rolling across the floor. Up ahead he saw a wall plunging through the floor, with another wall following from above.

He dived through the fleeting gap into the next room, then twisted to see Mr Banter trip against the plant pot. The orderly's grin vanished and he fell towards the room's edge. His arm reached through the gap between the disappearing wall and the one still coming. Cyan saw the plummeting wall meet his elbow.

There was a loud, fleshy crack. Cyan winced and kept moving, but reeled when the room he was in lifted and pushed his stomach against his pelvis. He floundered on a rug, no longer knowing which way was up, left, down or right, until the room stopped with a jolt. A flash of sky caught his eye – one of the sanctuary's deep, circular windows.

He ran towards it, but stopped at the cusp of the room he was in. The outer wall and its window were separated from Cyan by a room's worth of empty space.

"No-zone," breathed Cyan. He looked down to see a bedroom beneath the cube-shaped emptiness, with its window directly below the one he was facing.

"For Jonquil," he breathed, leaping into the no-zone. With a sliding ceiling skimming his hair, he plummeted into the room below and crashed onto its bed. Rolling off its mattress, he stumbled to the window, then began shuffling crablike to the right, to keep the window within reach while the floor slid left.

He jumped into the cavity and – after fumbling at the latch – slammed open the window and thrust his head into cool air.

# HEARTBEAT

Cyan almost wailed with relief; he was just two floors up, not far from the sanctuary's hangar.

He slipped while lowering himself onto the window frame below and fell with a thump onto sandy flagstones. But he was up immediately, limping as quickly as he could towards the sanctuary's front. The clouds raced with him. Angry gales sent sand hissing against windows.

When he took the corner he spied someone ahead: a shaded figure, squatting in the nook where the marble steps met the ground floor.

Keeping low, Cyan hobbled cautiously closer, then realized the figure was Teal, hunched up with his knees tucked beneath his chin.

Cyan increased his pace, slid to his knees and gripped Teal's elbow. "Teal!" he gasped. "Did you hear?"

"Hear what?" Teal peered up the side of the stairway,

in the direction of the revolving glass door. His eyes bulged with panic. "I was coming in from the harbour. Saw through the door…" He clutched the hand Cyan held to his elbow. "Have you seen what's happening up there? Orderlies are piling up on residents. Stabbing them with…*things*!" He glanced again towards the doorway. "What's going on, Cyan?"

Cyan squeezed his eyes shut, pushing away the mental image of what was happening in the foyer. When he opened them again, he saw Teal put a fingernail to his teeth. He could feel him quaking beneath his blazer.

"It's…a long story," panted Cyan. "But basically…Dr Haven's a psycho. He's been using us all as lab rats for a dangerous experiment."

Teal spat away some fingernail. "*What?* That's some sort of joke, right?"

"I wish it was."

"But Dr Haven…looks after us."

Cyan pointed at the top of the stairs. "Is that what he's doing up there?"

Teal bit his lip. His spectacles were crooked on his nose. "Oh, man…"

"It's okay," said Cyan, doing his best to reassure Teal. "There might be a way to stop him."

"Really?"

"I just need to get to the lift. If I can reach it, I might be able to end this. The foyer's rammed with orderlies, though, including one who's guarding the entrance. I don't know how to get past them all."

Teal gaped at Cyan, until his brow began to sink. "Hang on. How come you know all this stuff? Is it something to do with…you and Ruby being so weird lately?"

Cyan's lips clenched. "Yeah. It is."

"So you've known about Dr Haven for, like, a while or something?"

"I…guess so?"

*"Why didn't you tell me?"*

Cyan was flinching. "I'm so sorry, Teal. We weren't sure how you'd take it."

Teal's trembling eased off a little. He narrowed his eyes. "And why's that? Because I stress about stuff? This is worth some *serious* stressing, Cyan."

"Yeah. It is." Cyan put his hands on Teal's knees. "Listen. There's something I want to tell you right now, in case we're caught and forget everything."

"Forget everything?"

Cyan took a shaky breath. "I'm sorry, Teal, for all the times I made fun of you – for all your worrying and stuff. Honestly, I really am. I never thought about how hard it must actually be for you."

Teal didn't respond. His eyes were set on Cyan's face.

Cyan went on. "I know now. I know how your worry

goes deeper than you realize – how it comes from sadness and fear and things you don't even know you're feeling."

Teal's trembling had stopped. He stared open-mouthed at Cyan. "What?"

Cyan tightened his grip on Teal's knees. "You had every right to worry, Teal, and making fun of it was the last thing we should have done. We should have asked you about it. We should have *talked* to you. But this place…" He glared up at the sanctuary's cold face. "This place doesn't like that sort of talk. That's why it's so dangerous – why we all need to get away from here." His eyes went to the marble steps. "But we can't. Not unless I get to that lift."

Teal pushed Cyan's hands from his knees. His tone was hurt but his face looked stern. "What if I help?"

Cyan stared at him. "You think you can get to the lift?"

Teal huffed. "No way. I've got no idea what that lift's all about. Whatever you're planning is probably dangerous and stupid and that's your territory." He glanced to one side. "But I'm thinking…maybe you can reach the lift if everyone's distracted."

"Distracted?"

"I could run in the opposite direction, towards Ms Ferryman's office. I won't get far, but it might be enough to keep everyone's eyes off you."

Cyan frowned while giving this some thought. "You know what? That might actually work. They all think I'm in the upper rooms too; they wouldn't expect me to go through the front entrance."

His gaze rose, with something like awe, to Teal. He was beginning to regret ever doubting him. "You really want to do this?"

"No. Not in a million years. But it's that or…something way worse, right?"

"Right."

"So let's do it. Before I realize it's a terrible mistake."

After wiping his sweaty palms against his trousers, Teal groaned and got up. His voice was hoarse. "It's Teal time."

Cyan almost smiled, until he saw how Teal was trembling again. Mouthing a silent *thank you*, he skulked behind him and crouched at the bottom of the steps. He watched his friend ascend.

Teal paused by the revolving door, turning for a last look at Cyan. His wire glasses were wonky, but the eyes behind them were fiercer than Cyan had ever known.

After taking in a breath – a breath so deep and long that it straightened his back – Teal barged the glass door and entered.

With the wind whipping behind him, Cyan followed on all fours. The hem of his blazer slid along marble steps, and when he neared the top, he peered through the spinning glass. He caught sight of Teal in the foyer, sprinting to the right with his arms flailing, bellowing something Cyan couldn't hear.

All eyes – including those of Dr Haven, who was standing with Ms Ferryman by the staircase – were on Teal.

Cyan made his move.

Ignoring the pain in his ankles and thighs, he stooped and ran, first slinking through the still-spinning door, then darting to the left, past some wrestling staff and residents, straight to the corridor that led to the lift.

Mr Banter's card was already in his hand. He swiped it, leaped through the lift's parting doors, slammed in the code – three-one-one-two – and almost collapsed when the doors closed.

The lift descended. When its doors opened Cyan was on the move again. He ran past the corridor of cells straight to Ruby, who was still out cold on the dirty floor. He winced at the bruise that blotted half her neck, then stooped with an ear to her nostrils. Her breathing was steady.

He pulled off his blazer, folded it into a pillow and tucked it tenderly beneath Ruby's head. After brushing her cheek with his fingertips he was up again, limping back to the corridor he'd passed.

Cyan moved as quickly as he could down the corridor's length, slowing at each door to swipe Mr Banter's card. He left a trail of green lights in his wake, heard the echoing clicks of unlocking doors.

"Come out!" he cried. "It's okay! You can all come out! You're safe now! You're safe!"

He'd reached the corridor's end and turned around to see two doors opening. A teenage boy and girl – both wilting and garbed in grey gowns – stepped gingerly from their rooms. They cowered and blinked in the grimy, flickering light.

"It's okay," repeated Cyan, his voice quieter. "Come on. Don't be scared. We're getting you out."

Gradually, more doors opened. The corridor began to fill up.

Some of the residents were so young. They stumbled and squinted, gradually turning their heads to Cyan. One of them – a bald girl who looked about ten, with medical gauze taped to the side of her head – fixed him with dull green eyes.

With that familiar sting pricking his eyelids, Cyan smiled at her. The girl's lips moved. Her expression was thin, tremoring, weak. But it was there, and it was almost a smile.

Cyan headed back down the corridor, squeezing gently between residents. He stopped, though, after brushing past someone with a bob of blonde hair.

"Amber?" He made to step towards her then faltered. His heart ached when she flinched and backed away. "Or… Ruth, right? Ruth McMurphy. It's you. I found your code.

And your note. I…" He trailed off at the confusion in her eyes. She had no idea what he was talking about.

"It's all right." Cyan fought the quiver in his smile and kept moving, until the sight of thin arms and black hair stopped him in his tracks.

"Jonquil," he breathed.

She turned slowly and her dark gaze shifted – not to Cyan, but to the empty space in front of him.

"Jonquil?" he repeated.

She didn't respond. Her eyes didn't move.

"Don't worry," whispered Cyan. "You're going to be fine." He took a timid step towards her and – opening his arms very, very slowly – embraced her as softly as he could.

Jonquil didn't move. Not by a millimetre. But Cyan could feel her heartbeat, strong and alive and quickening against his chest.

Again, the pinpricks behind his eyes. He blinked several times, exhaled and stepped away.

"Okay!" Heads began to turn. Cyan was beckoning towards the lift. "Hop in, everyone. There's room if we squeeze together. I need you upstairs."

# GREY PARADE

Cyan entered a foyer far quieter than the one he'd left. Residents were sprawled across the floor and propped up on benches. Orderlies worked silently and methodically, hauling unconscious bodies onto cold metal trolleys.

Dr Haven was still by the spiral staircase, to the right of the foyer's handless clock. He wore a rigid frown, with his face a dark and unfamiliar shade of pink.

Abruptly he broke the silence, calling irritably into his locket. "Mr Banter! Send me an update this instant!"

"I doubt he can hear you," Cyan replied.

The director lifted his head, his eyes growing wide at the sight of Cyan. He gaped at the spiral staircase behind him, then looked again at Cyan. "How…" Another glance at the stairs. "Where's Mr Banter?"

The orderlies had stopped their work to watch.

"Still up there," said Cyan. "Somewhere."

The doctor's eyes narrowed into slits. "Orderlies. Take him immediately."

Two orderlies not far from Cyan reached into their pockets, and within a blink were wielding needles.

"Wait." Cyan put a palm up to them. "You might want to see this."

Turning around, he gestured towards the corridor. He moved backwards while he beckoned, to make way for the residents from below.

While they shuffled into the foyer, Cyan saw orderlies' expressions changing. Some of them looked baffled, while others became as stiff and pale as their uniforms.

Cyan joined the freed residents, who'd stopped and huddled together as if for warmth. Many of them were wincing and blinking again, struggling with the foyer's brighter light.

Cyan's gaze swept the orderlies. When he spoke it was to Ms Ferryman. "Do any of these faces look familiar?"

Ms Ferryman's mouth opened, closed, then opened again. She seemed unable to speak, but eventually managed a nod.

She turned to Dr Haven, who was backing silently away. His lips twitched at their edges, and he'd paled from pink to skull-grey. But he flushed again, stopped and stood his ground.

"I said take him immediately!" he bellowed, glowering at his staff.

Some of the orderlies avoided his gaze. One of them shook her head. But others were steeling themselves, readying their needles.

The slide of soles against carpet. Cyan followed the sound; two orderlies had blocked the exit. Others came from the front and sides, closing in.

"Orderlies, stand down!" It was Ms Ferryman, who'd left the stairway to join Cyan. She glanced sidelong to meet his eye, then held a stern finger up to her staff.

The advancing orderlies hesitated, their eyes flitting to Dr Haven.

"Don't listen to her!" he barked. "I'm your *superior*!"

"And he's a liar!" countered Ms Ferryman.

Even by her steeliest standards, her expression was grim. She peered over her shoulder at the residents bunched up behind her, then returned her attention to her staff. "You know these children as well as I do. Dr Haven said they'd recovered and were safely back home again. Do they *look* recovered to you? Didn't they just come out of that lift?"

"Ignore this nonsense!" snapped Dr Haven. "Take them all down and Ms Ferryman too or…or suffer the consequences!"

Some of the orderlies turned their faces from the doctor to the floor. Cyan saw a cartridge fall from someone's hand. But a handful of orderlies were still looking at the director.

Their jaws and shoulders tightened. With needles poised and glinting, they crept forward again.

"Consequences?" croaked Cyan. He waved an arm at the quaking residents. "*These*...are the consequences, if you keep listening to the doctor. Just look at them! Look at their faces and *remember*! Don't you remember them the way they were before?"

He saw Amber cowering behind Ms Ferryman. She looked so afraid, with her face pinched and pale beneath her scruffy bob. "Look at Amber!" he went on. "*I* don't remember her before she was like this – before she was *withdrawn* and hidden away. But I'm sure most of you do!"

With their eyes on Amber, all except one of the approaching orderlies slowed and stayed put.

The one still edging closer – a young male orderly fairly new to the sanctuary – glanced at Dr Haven, before stepping forward at another nod from the director.

He faltered, though, when someone emerged from the huddle. It was Jonquil. She stared at him with eyes deep and brown, childlike and unblinking.

Cyan spoke to the orderly, his voice softer now. "You're new here, aren't you? You probably don't know these residents. But you knew Jonquil, right? You remember how she was. Before the doctor did this to her. This is what you've been part of, without even knowing. It's what you'll *still* be part of, unless you stay where you are and lower that syringe."

The orderly's lips creased, and he lowered his eyes. He held his cartridge out to Ms Ferryman, who stepped forward to take it from his hand.

Cyan was limping past orderlies, on direct course to Dr Haven. Every eye in the foyer went to the director. Some orderlies had shifted into new positions; once again all exits were blocked.

Cyan paused by a trolley when he saw Teal unconscious on its top. He rested a grateful hand on his friend's chest, as proud of him as he was sorry, then continued on his way.

The doctor stood trembling with rage. He glared at Cyan with silent, seething contempt.

"Ahoy." Cyan's voice was hoarse. He wiped his face with the sleeve of his shirt.

Ms Ferryman joined him. Cyan eyed the syringe still in her hand. "Shall we give the doctor a taste of his own medicine?"

Ms Ferryman nodded; Cyan stepped aside. Dr Haven twitched on the spot, making to flee. But there was nowhere to go.

The doctor looked so helpless – so thin and frightened – as two orderlies took his arms. But when the needle entered his arm, he fixed his cold, grey eyes on Cyan.

Cyan had never felt so drained. It took all of his strength to lift his finger to his head. Unable even to smile, he saluted the slumping director: a tired tap of an imaginary cap.

RECOVERY PHASE A

# SALTWATER

The walls rattled with the thrum of spinning blades.

Cyan watched through the side window of the sanctuary's helicopter, saw dunes racing by below. Even from up here, cutting through the sky at over a hundred knots per hour, the sands were relentless.

He peered to the west. The sun was plump and poised on the horizon. A handful of clouds, with golden curls on their swollen bellies, speckled a peach-hued sky.

Cyan edged closer to the window, to watch the convoy of helicopters that flew alongside his own. Most were military: soaring green Chinooks, with propellers at both ends. But there were other helicopters too. Black ones, unmarked, with sharp noses and tinted windows. And Cyan could see two air ambulances – metallic red and neon yellow – speeding side by side within the thundering flock.

And inside every helicopter: residents in gowns and

uniforms, taking leave of the Elsewhere Sanctuary.

He turned from the window to look at Teal, Jonquil and Ruby. They were sitting at the centre of the cabin on the webbed seating that faced the cockpit. Teal and Ruby were on either side of Jonquil, who was gazing blankly ahead.

Teal seemed dazed, with eyes pink and sleepy behind his crooked glasses; it had only been a few hours since residents were being tranquilized in the foyer. He cupped one of Jonquil's hands and said something to her, though Cyan couldn't hear over the helicopter's hum.

Ruby saw Cyan watching, smiled tiredly, and crossed the cabin to join him on the seat by the window.

Cyan grimaced at the bruise on her neck, which was beginning to dull from blue to purple. He leaned in close, so she could hear him over the drone. "You okay?"

"Shipshape."

A huffed laugh left Cyan's nose. "How's Jonquil?"

"Hardly the life and soul of the party. But she's responding, I think. Moving sort of…quicker, too. That's progress, right?" She peered uneasily at Jonquil. "Do you think she'll get back to the way she was?"

"Fingers crossed. I'm hoping a bit of kindness'll do more than strobes and syringes."

Ruby nodded to herself, then turned her head to the cockpit. Cyan followed her gaze, and saw sunset filling the pilot's visor.

"What about Ms Ferryman and Professor Vadasz?" It was Ruby, close to his ear. "Are they on these helicopters?"

Cyan shook his head. "The professor is, but Ms Ferryman's staying. She went to the hidden floor with a bunch of people who were flashing IDs at each other – the same ones who took Dr Haven away. Said she wants to make sure our files go to people who can help us. I heard her saying something to one of those suited types, about digging through records to find out who was funding the sanctuary and helping Dr Haven."

"I guess he's is in big trouble."

"The bigger the better."

Ruby moved suddenly to the window. Her finger was pressed against the plexiglass. "Look at that!"

Cyan leaned to look. Ruby was pointing at something huge, black and oblong that protruded from several dunes. He thought it might be some sort of whale, until he saw metallic fins and a propeller. "Is that…"

"A submarine." Ruby was grinning at the sight. Her knee began to jiggle. "Wow, right?"

"Yeah. Wow." Cyan kept his eyes to the dunes. He wasn't sure, but there seemed to be a gradual shifting in the sandscape. The dunes looked flatter, somehow. And the boats they passed – rusted wrecks and metal husks – were few and far between. Something flashed in the softening light: the beached corpse of a giant jellyfish.

They both fell silent, watching the sands pass beneath them.

"So…" began Ruby. Her voice caught in her throat.

Cyan looked across. Ruby's smile was gone.

"We're going back," she said. "No more Island of Elsewhere. We're all going to be…somewhere. It's kind of scary, right?"

She looked nervously at Cyan. Her curls were wilder than ever. "All the stuff we left behind," she said. "All the stuff Dr Haven lured us away from… I guess we'll have to face up to it."

Cyan's eyelids began to tingle. "Yeah. I guess we will." He watched Ruby bite her bottom lip, so hard that it must have hurt. "Are you scared?"

Ruby swallowed. "Yeah. I am. I mean…" She balled up her hands. "I know running away got us into this mess. And I know keeping everything pent up has been…hurting us." She threw a glance at Jonquil, before looking again at Cyan. He could see the fear in her eyes.

"But what…" she began. "What if going back hurts us too? It's bound to, isn't it? We've all run away from horrendous, traumatic things. You can see it in the oaths on our lockets. All that pain we had, before Dr Haven removed it."

Cyan shook his head. "Dr Haven never removed it. He only hid it. He stopped us from dealing with it. From ever having the chance to heal."

"Well, yeah. Sure. But what if going back is even worse? Maybe it'll damage us even more than the sanctuary?"

At first, Cyan didn't know how to answer, so he took one of Ruby's trembling fists, eased it open, and held her hand in his own.

And then he knew.

He brushed a curl from her cheek. "I'm sorry, Ruby. I can't answer that. I don't know what it was you went through. And I don't know what you're going back to. But I do know that whatever it is, no matter how much it hurts, you won't face it alone. Just like I won't face my past alone. We'll help each other. Just like we'll help Jonquil, and all the others too."

Ruby fell silent. Moments passed by, until Cyan felt her squeeze his hand.

"Yeah," she said. "We'll help each other." She managed a small smile. "And you'll get your parents back. Just like you wanted."

Cyan had to look away. "Not my mum. She's not alive anymore."

He heard Ruby take in a sudden, clipped breath. "Oh god... Cyan, I..."

"She died. After saving me from a fire." Cyan winced as the heat rushed in. It felt as if the fire that took his mother was in his head, burning behind his eyes. "That's what... brought me to the sanctuary."

Ruby's palms folded over his hand. "I'm so sorry, Cyan."

"That's what it was." Cyan clamped his eyes shut. "The hurt that was always there, all along." His eyelids tremored. "At least I've got a chance of dealing with it now. I'm going to start by remembering Mum. So I'll get her back…in a way. And I won't lose her again. Not ever."

"What about your dad?"

"He's alive. Dr Haven said he started drinking and sort of…drew away." Cyan opened his eyes. They stung as if being pricked by pins.

"But I can see it now," he went on. "My dad was only doing what I did. Escaping. Hiding. Maybe I can find him."

Ruby squeezed his fingers. "I hope so. Whatever happens, I've got your back. Just like you've got mine. Like you said: we'll face it all together. No more hiding. More living."

Cyan nodded. "More living."

Ruby squeezed his fingers again, softer this time. "Hey…"

"Yeah?"

"Do you remember when you took me to the *Serenity*, to show me those lipstick pictures? When you said you'd asked me to help 'cos it felt…right?"

Cyan swallowed the painful bulge in his throat. "Yeah. I remember."

"And I said I didn't know what you meant."

Cyan nodded. Ruby's hand pulled away.

"I know now," she said. "I know what you meant. About it feeling right."

She put her arms around him and rested her warm curls against his neck. Cyan embraced her too, then opened his eyes. Something in the window had changed; a play of light on the plexiglass.

He shifted gently to look down and saw rolling blue waves. It was the sea, sparkling and vast, sand turned to water.

Cyan blinked through his glasses, pulled in by the foaming waves. He felt suddenly adrift, lost in their languid loll and rhythm – in their turquoise beauty, their white-crested freedom.

"Ruby…" he whispered.

Ruby looked down and – for a moment – stopped breathing.

While Cyan watched the rolling waves, he felt not only sadness and sorrow, but also laughter and hope, mingling in the salt-stream that ran from his eyes. The ache ebbed away, and the burn lost its sting. Tears ran like balm down his cheeks.

For finally, he could cry.

"Guys," said Ruby, beckoning the others.

Teal got up and guided Jonquil to the window.

And all four of them stared as one, enthralled by a glittering horizon.

# AUTHOR'S NOTE

I have a car crash to thank for this book. That, and my determination to turn lemons into lemonade.

One day, while driving my eldest son home from swimming, I crashed into the back of another car. It was completely my fault. A moment's daydreaming – that's all it took. Thankfully no one was hurt.

Even so, I was racked with guilt and found myself obsessing over how much worse things could have been. My son had been with me, and two people were in the other car. What if my carelessness had hurt someone? I felt like an idiot, and my self-esteem sank quicker than I'd ever imagined possible.

As hard as the experience was, I promised myself I'd use it as inspiration for my next book. And while coming to terms with what happened, one thing really struck me: how much it helped to talk.

I'd tried hard to deal with my guilt. I punished myself by not seeing friends, and googled car crashes every day, searching for statistics that might make me feel better. I knew I was overreacting but I couldn't help it.

But nothing worked like talking to people. When I grumbled to my family and friends, they reassured me and offered love and perspective. They'd listen and nod, sharing stories of how they'd been through similar things.

Sharing through talking can be so helpful. It allows you to see that you're not alone, and that making a mistake doesn't make you a bad person. The kindness of others makes you kinder to yourself.

Openness. Communication. Empathy. Connection. These are so crucial for getting us over life's bumps.

On the flip side there's refusing to talk about your problems; avoiding difficult emotions and not telling others the truth about how you feel. But trying to cope alone and keeping your worries bottled up can make you feel worse in the long run.

So, that's what I decided to write about. And with that in mind, *The Memory Thieves* took shape.

Ignoring negative feelings can be tempting, of course. And when you're suffering, there's a lot to be said for escape and distraction. But hiding away isn't always ideal, so I developed a setting that allowed me to explore its risks. It made sense to use a faraway island, and this became the

Island of Elsewhere: a place that promises the purest escape, even from the memory of your old life.

Like many authors, I'm a magpie. I gathered trinkets and ideas and combined them to create the island and its Elsewhere Sanctuary. Many ideas came while holidaying on the Yorkshire coast with my family – while losing my bearings, for example, in the back corridors of Scarborough's Grand Hotel, and realizing how getting lost might help those who want to lose themselves. Or researching not only New York's Maritime Hotel, but also sliding puzzle cubes, and combining the two into a building that regularly shifts so its residents never quite know where they are. A building with no hands on its clocks, so that time is as vague as space.

I also remember watching the tide leave the coastal town of Staithes and wondering what it would be like if it never came back. It felt like a fitting symbol for a place of disconnection and separation from emotions, so I drew inspiration from the Aral Sea – a huge lake that's been shrinking for decades, leaving boats stranded on its dunes.

I magpied other things too. Stylings from an old 60s TV show called *The Prisoner*. Genuine experimental methods being used to alter memories. The Costa Concordia – a cruise ship that sank before being raised from the sea. And then I added the novel's central characters: some plucky but troubled teens, and a sinister doctor.

What I ended up with was *The Memory Thieves*. Lemonade from lemons. The silver lining on my car's crumpled bonnet.

I hope you enjoyed reading this book as much as I enjoyed writing it. But most of all, I hope it inspires you to talk about your doubts and fears, to let out your feelings, and to be kind to others when they do the same.

Showing weakness is one of the bravest things anyone can do.

Darren Simpson, 2021

# TALKING ABOUT FEELINGS

At the heart of *The Memory Thieves* is a message of hope: that everyone feels emotions they find difficult, and that we all experience events that make us sad, angry or scared. This book is a reminder that we are all capable of dealing with negative experiences and, with the support and help of friends and family, need not be afraid of sharing those experiences, and finding our way back to happiness.

Here are some exercises and talking points, devised by a psychologist who specialises in helping young people through challenging experiences and emotions. We hope these will help you open up and talk about your feelings, too. You can do these exercises with friends, or with your parents, guardians, or other family members.

- Make a list of some of the feelings or emotions you have experienced. We'll start with some obvious ones, but can you think of some others? For example, happiness, sadness, worry, excitement.

- Pick one of the feelings you have listed. Can you remember what you notice about yourself when you are feeling this way? What does your body feel like? What do other people notice about you when you are experiencing that emotion? Can you think about how it makes you feel when you realize someone else is experiencing that emotion?

- Who are the people you can talk to about your emotions? Think about the adults in your life you trust and feel safe and comfortable talking about tricky feelings with. For example, parents, older siblings, uncles and aunts, cousins, grandparents and teachers.

- It's always okay to have feelings, and all feelings are important. Sometimes it can be useful to think about ways we can let people know how we are feeling. Consider the emotions you have listed, and think about how you might communicate you are experiencing these, especially if that feeling is bothering you.

- Sometimes it's easiest to just say how you feel, for example; "I feel frustrated". Sometimes you might want to write your feelings down. Sometimes you might want to draw an angry face and stick it on the fridge. Or perhaps you just want to run around outside and feel free. You might even be tempted to dance!

- If you're doing these exercises with a grown-up, what would you like them to do when you tell them about your feelings?

Share the following text with a grown-up.

*Grown-ups, as your young reader considers each of their feelings, can you help them to think about the physical things they notice about themselves when they are experiencing that feeling? Share with them what you notice about them when they are feeling a certain way. Tell them how certain emotions make you feel and behave too.*

*And grown-ups, sometimes our young people just want us to listen to them and remind them that it's okay to feel that way. Sometimes they want help to feel more calm. Sometimes they want help to work out what to do. And sometimes, something can't be fixed or changed, and it just has to be accepted. And that's okay, too.*

- Sometimes feelings can get so tricky, or so big, that you and your grown-up might need help from trained psychologists or doctors. (Don't worry, they won't be like Dr Haven!) These doctors are specially trained, and have rules that they must follow in order to help you. In most cases, this help comes in the form of talking about your feelings, and coming up with ways of dealing with them. Sometimes, children might need medication as part of their treatment (and don't worry, it's nothing like the pills in *The Memory Thieves*!).

- Above all, if you have a feeling, a memory or a thought that is upsetting you, whatever it is, have a think about it, notice it, and share it by talking with a loved one. It's the best way to get to know yourself, each other, and your feelings.

# DISCUSSION
# QUESTIONS

1. Think about the power of names in the novel. How might the residents be affected by having their real names replaced with colours? Do the names of the adult characters give any clues about their roles in the story?

2. "What you don't know can't hurt you." Do you think this saying is true? Is it true for the characters in *The Memory Thieves*?

3. Look up the word "sanctuary" in a dictionary. Do you think the Elsewhere Sanctuary deserves its name? If not, what would you call it and why?

4.  Look at the first three pages of the novel. How does Darren Simpson create a sense of place in *The Memory Thieves*? How does this help to prepare the reader for the story to come?

5.  "We don't do time here." Why do you think Dr Haven has removed all sense of time from the residents of the Elsewhere Sanctuary? How do you think you would cope in a world where you never knew the time?

6.  Think about the nautical references in *The Memory Thieves* – the anchor logo, the greeting "ahoy!", the doffing of imaginary sailors' hats, the *Serenity*. Why do you think the author has chosen to include these? Consider the significance of the ocean in the novel.

7.  What do you think happens to Cyan and his friends after the end of the novel? How might they cope with going back to "the real world", and learning about their pasts?

8.  How does the author portray the character of Dr Haven in *The Memory Thieves*? What do you think makes for a good villain in a story?

9. Look at the passage on pages 85-86, showing the memories Ruth McMurphy recorded on the *Serenity*. Why do you think she chose these details to write down? If you could only save a few memories, what would they be?

10. What genre, or mix of genres, best describes *The Memory Thieves*, and why?

11. Have you read Darren Simpson's author's note? In it, he explains that he wrote *The Memory Thieves* after a car accident made him realize the importance of talking about your problems. How does this theme appear in the novel?

12. "Can you imagine how much people will pay to have their worst memories removed?" If the Lethe Method was possible, do you think people would actually pay for it? Would you?

13. Other than strobe therapy and medication, what measures are used at the Sanctuary to disorientate residents? How do you think these things impact the children's memories?

14. Compare the first (pages 47-51) and last (pages 271-274) reconfigurations in the book. How does this turn from something that seems like a fun adventure, into something more sinister?

15. Turn to page 297, the very end of the novel, and reread the last page. How did you feel while reading this ending? Why do you think the author chose to end the story at this point?

# ACKNOWLEDGEMENTS

I'm so blessed to have my scribblings end up in your hands, dear reader, and would like to thank the following people not only for supporting me, but also for making the world a brighter place. Soppy, I know, and the cheese-fest that follows will induce much further retching. But I mean every word.

Eternal thanks to Wanda, my wonderful wife – my anchor and my buoy. Times have been strange, but it says a lot that they've brought us even closer. Thank you, Wanda, for the faith you've always had in me.

And thank you to Oskar and Charlie, who constantly amuse and amaze me. You boys know I'm joking when I say you're only cute when you're asleep; I adore you every moment of every day.

Sending love and gratitude to my mum and dad, Sue and Graham, for being awesome parents and equally awesome grandparents. Love also to Elvis, Kelly and Graham, to their sidekicks and spawnlings, and to my wider family and in-laws. One more Salmiakki, Erhard?

Thanks to Ol Bailey, *The Memory Thieves'* first ever young reader, for their honesty, thoroughness and enthusiasm. I couldn't have asked for a better guinea pig.

I can't thank my agent, Laura Susijn, enough. Thank you, Laura, for sticking with me when waters were choppy, and for always having my back.

High-fives (up above) to Stephanie King, my editor extraordinaire, for truly understanding my stories, and for bringing out the best in what I do. You make coal into diamonds, Stephanie!

And high fives (down below) to Sarah Stewart for editing prowess and quality control.

Throwing further high-fives in the direction of Jenny Glencross for her kind words and copyedits, to Charlotte Forfieh and Alice Moloney for their meticulous proofreading (and for those shrewd discussion points, Alice!), and to Sarah Cronin for her very elegant typesetting.

Deep gratitude goes to Usborne's Publicity Manager, Kat Jovanovic, for her patience and counsel while I got to grips with this author malarkey. And thanks to Jessica Feichtlbauer and Joanna Olney for the fanfare and ballyhoo.

Thank you to Matt Saunders for capturing the Island of Elsewhere so atmospherically on this book's cover, and to Will Steele for his sterling taste and art direction.

Giddy whoops go out to the Class of '18: Samuel J. Halpin, A.M. Howell and Serena Patel. It's been a joy to watch you grow, guys. Thanks for all the therapy and laughs.

I'd like to sing the praises of Usborne's Books at Home posse, who offer more zeal and support than an author could wish for. Special shout-outs to Susannah Hobbs, Dionne Lakey,

Charlene Riviere, Sara Sumner and Katy Wedderburn.

To everyone else at Usborne HQ or working with them: thank you! It truly takes a village to raise a novel.

To Dr Aayesha Mulla and Leila Rasheed: I am in your debt. Thank you for your time and expertise, and for giving *The Memory Thieves* such illuminating sensitivity reads.

I fell into children's fiction somewhat by accident, and quickly discovered that the kidlit community is one of the best in the world. I'd like to thank all the teachers, librarians, authors, artists, bloggers, reviewers, tweeters, Instagrammers, YouTubers, booksellers, booklovers, charities and champions for the parts they play. Honourable mentions go to Jess Alex, Andrew Bailie, David Barker, Colin Baxter, the Bengaluru Sustainability Forum, Jasbinder Bilan, Resa Boenard, the Book Whisperer (I hope this was worth the wait, Tris!), Alison Brumwell, Jo Clarke, Mariesa Dulak, Christopher Edge, Jonathan Emmett, Empathy Lab, Kitty Empire, Scott Evans, Lily Fae, the Federation of Children's Book Groups, Sarah Forestwood, Christopher Frost, Lucy Georgeson, James Haddell, Ben Harris, the Honest Bookworm, Emily Landsborough, Inspire Libraries, Tracy Lowe, Mabel (check out those glasses!), Megan Nicholson, Oxford University Press, Kate Poels, the Reading Realm, Read It Daddy, the Rocketship Bookshop, Imogen Russell Williams, Liz Scott, Andy Shepherd, Chris Soul, Tima, Javad Tizmaghz, Samantha Thomas, Carol Williams, Alex Wheatle and VIP Reading.

Yes, the roll call above is absurdly long, but it only scratches the surface. To everyone involved in getting books to young readers: I salute you!

A little closer to home, thank you to Jim Alexander, Phil Formby, Kirsty Fox and Dan Layton of Bees Make Honey, always and forever. An extra ta goes to Dan for his superlative *Memory Thieves* portraits.

Hugs to my most musical friends, Chris Baldwin, Christophe Dejous, Richard Dytch, Matt Eris, Jason Holt, Neil Johnson, Graham Langley, Neil Marsden, Gavin McFarlane, Kieran O'Riordan and Mark Spivey.

Hello to Sandeep Mahal, Leanne Moden, Matt Turpin and all at Nottingham City of Literature, and to Lynne Towle, Julia Paynton, Marykate McGrath and co of the Literacy Trust's Read On Nottingham hub. Thank you for promoting Nottingham's writers and supporting the literacy of its children.

Thanks also to Ross Bradshaw, Pippa Hennessy and the other book sages at Five Leaves Bookshop, and to Polis Loizou and the team at Waterstones Nottingham.

I'm saving my biggest THANK YOU! for all the children and teens I've met since starting this journey. Thank you to each and every one of you, for the hope you give me for the future.

One final thing. The idea for *The Memory Thieves* rose from the debris of a car crash. So thank you, L, for being so gracious after I accidentally hit your car. You were right: it made us stronger.

When the truth hit Bren, it was as cold and hard as the frost on the window: if he didn't get out of here, he'd die.

It was plain fact. A message to the gut, sent from Bren's tingling toes and hands. His fingers stung as if being pricked by pins of ice, so he hugged himself and shoved his hands beneath his armpits, trying to stop the shivering. But the harder he squeezed himself, the more he shook.

He'd left school about an hour ago; there was still some daylight outside. But not for long. The February sun was sinking. Its pale light barely made it into the room, oozing through the metal grate that covered the window.

But there was light enough to see. Bren pivoted on the torn, filthy carpet, checking for anything he might have missed, anything that might get him out.

There was the stained mattress, propped against the wall. A radiator, with magnolia paint peeling from its metal. The grated window, looking down upon Bradbury Avenue. And Bren's school backpack, sitting on the floor.

But that was all. There was nothing that could smash through the window. Nothing that could get him through the locked door or even dent its wood.

Bren returned to the window to pound again with his fists – to rap with his knuckles until they bled. He shouted at the glass, crying out for help, though his throat was raw from all the shouting he'd done already.

It was pointless. Even if his voice carried through the double glazing, no one would hear. No one lived on Bradbury Avenue. It was no man's land. Every terraced house on it was the same. Boarded windows and bricked-up doors. Back gardens full of weeds and litter, nettles and junk.

Bren gave up. His fists left prints on the window, blotching its whorls of spiralling ice. Frost glossed the walls too. The dated floral wallpaper – speckled in places by mould – twinkled in cold, bluish light.

Bren's woolly gloves were on the floor; he'd taken them off to heave at the door and thump the window. Still shivering, Bren put them on and shuffled back to the door. He knew its lock was jammed but he tried again. He rattled and strained at the handle, pulling and pleading as if the door could hear him, then started kicking with his feet. But the door was too thick. It wouldn't budge from its frame.

Grunting hoarsely, Bren grabbed his backpack, pulled the mattress to the floor and sat down. He could feel the cold dampness seeping through his school trousers. His stomach ached in a way it had never ached before. He checked his backpack for something to eat, knowing as he rummaged that there was nothing. The food his dad had packed for him that morning was gone; he'd eaten it in the music room at lunchtime.

The thought of Dad made Bren's eyes well up. He'd be worried. Again.

Bren pulled his phone from his duffel coat, looked miserably at its cracked screen. Fifty per cent battery, but no signal at all. He was trapped.

But then again: maybe not.

Removing a glove again, Bren reached into his trouser pocket and pulled out a wristwatch. The room's silence amplified its steady ticking. It sounded like a knife on a chopping board, hacking the moments into seconds.

Squinting in the gloom, Bren studied the watch. Its olive-green face – set within a simple golden bezel – matched its green strap. There was a round gap at the face's centre, which exposed the cogs working beneath the dial.

Bren watched those golden, ticking hands. Nearly five o'clock.

He curled up on the mattress, put his ear to the watch and closed his eyes.

The ticking went on, lulling him softly. He could feel every tick, every tock, passing through his fingers, travelling up his arms, calming his heart.

Tick.

Tock.

Tick.

Tock.

And then he heard it. The clacking of cogs much larger than the watch's. He opened his eyes.

A section of carpet tightened, before splitting with a soft tearing sound. It parted to reveal a ring of spinning golden cogs, each one pulling at carpet threads to make the gap even wider.

A circle of polished wooden floor lay exposed by the parting threads. It opened up, like the sliding shutter of a camera lens.

Bright light and birdsong filled the room.

The birdsong of Furthermoor.

WELCOME TO AN UNFORGETTABLE
WORLD, IN THIS SPELLBINDING
ADVENTURE ABOUT THE
POWER OF THE IMAGINATION

# FURTHERMOOR
## COMING IN 2022